Aden, Arabie

Also available in the
Twentieth-Century Continental Fiction Series

Paul Nizan

Aden, Arabie

with a Foreword by Jean-Paul Sartre

translated from the French by Joan Pinkham

COLUMBIA UNIVERSITY PRESS   New York   1987

Columbia University Press Morningside Edition 1986
Columbia University Press
New York

Library of Congress Cataloging-in-Publication Data

Nizan, Paul.
  Aden, Arabie.

  (Twentieth-Century Continental fiction)
  I. Title. II. Series.
PQ2627.I95A6813 1987   843'.912   86-8943
ISBN 0-231-06357-1

This edition published by arrangement with Editions
la Découverte and the Monthly Review Foundation

Translator's Acknowledgments

For their kind assistance in identifying several of the allusions and quotations that appear in this book, I wish to thank Professor Henri Peyre of Yale University, Professor J. P. Coursodon of the City College of New York, Professors Jean Hytier and Michael Riffaterre of Columbia University, and Professor Serge Gavronsky of Barnard College.

I should also like to express my deep appreciation to Rodolphe L. Coigney, M.D., who checked many passages in the translation and without whose help it would have been a much more imperfect work.

J. P.

Foreword

by Jean-Paul Sartre

One day when Valéry was bored he walked over to the window, and staring into the transparent pane, asked, "How can a man hide?" Gide was present. Disconcerted by this studied laconicism, he said nothing. There were many possible replies, however: anything will serve to hide a man, from hunger and want to formal dinners, from the county jail to the Académie Française. But these two bourgeois celebrities had a high opinion of themselves. Every day they washed their twin souls in public and thought they were revealing the naked truth. When they died long after, one morose, the other satisfied, both in ignorance, they had not even harkened to the young voice that cried out for all of us, their descendants: "Where is man hiding? We are suffocating. They mutilate us from childhood. We are all monsters!"

It is not enough to say that the man who thus denounced our true situation suffered in the flesh. While he lived, not an hour passed but he ran the risk of ruin. Dead, he faced an even greater danger: to make him pay for his discernment, a bunch of moral cripples conspired to make all trace of him vanish.

He had belonged to the Party for twelve years when, in September 1939, he announced that he was leaving it. That was the unpardonable offense, the sin of despair that the Christian God punishes with damnation. But communists do not believe in hell, they believe in nothingness. It was decided that Comrade Nizan should be obliterated. He had already been hit in the back of the neck by a dumdum bullet, but this liquidation satisfied no one. It was not enough that he had ceased to live. He must never have existed at all. The Party members persuaded those who had witnessed his life that they had never really known him: he was a traitor, he had sold out; he had been in the pay of the Ministry of the Interior, where receipts had been found bearing his signature. A comrade took it upon himself to interpret the works he had left, and discovered in them an obsession to betray. How, said this philosopher, would an author who puts informers in his novels know anything about their ways unless he was one himself? A profound argument, as one can see, but a dangerous one—indeed, the interpreter himself later turned traitor and has just been thrown out of the Party. Should we thus accuse him of projecting his own obsessions onto his victim? In any case, the maneuver was successful: the suspicious books disappeared. The Communists intimidated the publishers, who left the books to rot in basements, and they intimidated readers, who no longer dared ask for them. This seed of silence would germinate. In ten years it would produce absolute negation. The dead man would be evicted from history, his name would fall to dust, his birth would be erased from our common past.

The Communists started with all the odds in their favor: any amateur can rifle a tomb at night in a poorly guarded cemetery. If they lost the first round, it was only because they had too much contempt for us. Blinded by mourning and by glory, the Party intellectuals decided they were an order of knighthood and privately referred to themselves as "the permanent heroes of our time." I think it was around this period that a former student of mine said to me with gentle irony, "You see, we Communist intellectuals suffer from a superiority complex." In a word, submen, unaware of their sub-humanity. They became so arrogant as to try their calumnies on Nizan's best friends as a sort of test. The results were conclusive. When we challenged them publicly to produce their proofs, they retreated in disorder, complaining that we never trusted them and that we weren't being nice.

It was we who lost the second round. To confound the enemy is nothing. We should have convinced them, pressed our advantage, cut off their retreat. But we were frightened by our victory —we really liked them at heart, these unjust soldiers of Justice. Someone said, "Let's not make an issue of it, or they'll get angry." We heard nothing more of the affair, but whispers made the rounds of the CP, and new recruits, in Bergerac, in Mazamet, learned dispassionately, without the shadow of a doubt, about the ancient crimes of somebody named Nizan.

When I think about it, our negligence seems suspicious. I am willing to grant that we really believed in good faith that the man's innocence had been re-established. But his works? Is there any excuse for having made no attempt to save them from oblivion? They had been meant to give offense—that was their greatest merit—and I am sure that even we found them offensive. I remember that we had acquired beautiful new souls, so beautiful that I still blush to think of it. The Nation, which wished to waste nothing, had decided to turn over to us the empty, insatiable pools it didn't know what to do with: the drowned pain, the unsatisfied demands of the deceased, in short everything that couldn't be salvaged. It conferred on us the virtues of its martyrs, we were decorated posthumously in our own lifetime. The honored dead, in sum. Everyone whispered that we were the Righteous. Smiling, cheerful, funereal, we took this lofty vacuity for fulfillment and hid our unprecedented promotion under the simplicity of our manners. Virtue—along with whisky—was our principal diversion. Friends with everybody! The enemy had invented classes to undo us; now that he was beaten, they disappeared with him. Workers, bourgeois, and peasants communed together in the holy love of Country. In authorized circles we believed that self-sacrifice pays cash, that crime doesn't pay, that the worst is not inevitable, and that moral progress advances technical progress. We proved by our very existence, and by our self-infatuation, that the wicked are always punished and the virtuous always rewarded. Covered with glory and at peace at last, the Left had entered the inexorable throes of death that thirteen years later would lay it in its grave to the sound of military fanfares, and we, poor fools, we thought it looked the picture of health. Soldiers and politicians who had come from England and Algeria were crushing the Resistance and stealing the Revolution before our very eyes, and we were writing in the newspapers and in our books that everything was going fine. Our souls had adopted for themselves the exquisite essence of these obliterated movements.

Nizan was a kill-joy. He issued a call to arms, to hatred. Class against class. With a patient and mortal enemy there can be no compromise: kill or be killed, there is nothing in between. And never sleep. All his life he had repeated, with his graceful insolence, looking down at his fingernails, "Don't believe in Santa Claus." He was dead, the war had just ended. By every French chimney shoes and boots had been set out, and Santa Claus was filling them with American canned goods. I am sure that at that time, those who started to leaf through *Aden* or *Antoine Bloyé* quickly laid the book aside with condescending pity: "Pre-war literature—simplistic and decidedly dated." What need had we of a Cassandra? We thought that if Nizan had lived he would have shared our new subtlety—that is, our compromises. What had preserved his violent purity? A stray bullet, that's all, nothing to brag about. This wretched dead man was quietly laughing his head off. He had written in his books that a French bourgeois past forty is nothing but a carcass. And then he had slipped away. At thirty-five. Now we, his classmates and comrades, puffed up with this flatulence we called our souls, reconciled with our enemies, were running about the public squares embracing everybody we met. And we were forty. Protecting the innocent, that was our business. We were the Just and we dispensed Justice. We left *Aden* in the hands of the Communists because we detested anyone who questioned our worth.

This attitude was punishable by law: refusal to come to the aid of a person in danger. If we did not liquidate our colleague morally, it was only because we were unable to. The rehabilitation was a farce; so was the interment. "Talk, talk, that's all you can do."* And we talked: our beautiful soul was the death of other men, our virtues were our absolute impotence. The truth is, it was up to the younger generation to revive Nizan the writer. But the young men of that time—quadragenarian carcasses today—didn't give it a thought. They had barely escaped an epidemic: what did this endemic disease, the bourgeois death, matter to them? Nizan asked them to turn inward just when

---

* The favorite remark of the parrot in Raymond Queneau's *Zazie dans le métro* (1959). (Trans.)

they thought they were finally going to be able to escape themselves. Oh, of course! they were going to die, Socrates is mortal, "Madame is dying, Madame is dead."* In school they had been made to memorize passages of celebrated works—Lamartine's *Le Lac*, a sermon by Bossuet. But there is a time for everything, and now it was time to live, since for five years they had thought they were going to die. As adolescents, they had been stunned by their country's defeat. They were miserable because they had lost all respect for everyone—for their fathers, and for the best army in the world, which had taken to its heels without fighting. The most generous among them had given themselves to the Party, which had given them everything in return: a sense of family, a monastic rule, a tranquil chauvinism, respectability. As soon as the war was over, these young people went mad with pride and humility. They took their pleasure in obedience. I have said that they despised us all—by way of compensation. They pinched their tomorrows till the blood came, to force them to sing. One can well imagine that the screeching of these birds drowned out the thin, chill voice of Nizan, the voice without tomorrow, the voice of death and eternity. Other adolescents relaxed happily in cellar nightclubs: they danced, they loved, they visited back and forth and held great rotating potlatches during which they threw their parents' furniture out the window. In a word, they did all that a young man can do. A few even read. Despairing, of course. All of them: it was the fashion. And they despaired of everything—except the vigorous pleasure of despairing. Except life. After five years their future was beginning to thaw. They had plans: the ingenuous hope of renewing literature through despair, of experiencing the awful dreariness of world travel, the insufferable boredom of earning money or seducing women, or, quite simply, of becoming a pharmacist, or a despairing dentist, and of living a long time, a very long time, with nothing to worry about except the human condition in general. How gay they were! Nizan had nothing to say to them. He spoke little

---

* A familiar quotation from Bossuet's funeral oration on Henriette-Anne d'Angleterre, Duchess of Orleans (1670). (Trans.)

about the human condition, a great deal about social matters and our alienations. He knew terror and rage rather than the sweetness of despair. In the young bourgeois with whom he associated he saw his own reflection and hated it—whether they were despairing or not, he despaired of them. His books were kept for the lean years, and rightly so.

Came the Marshall Plan. The Cold War struck a death-blow to this generation of dancers and vassals. As for the old-timers, we lost a few of our fine feathers, and all our virtues. "Crime does pay, you can get paid for crime." With the return of these fine maxims, our beautiful souls died stinking deaths. Good riddance. But the younger generation paid for us all. The nightclub rats turned into stupefied old young men. Some are turning gray, others are bald, others have put on a spare tire. Their relaxation has congealed into an inert void. They do what they have to do, in a modest way, they earn their living, they have a fine car, a country house, a wife and children. But hope and despair have taken wing together. These boys were just getting ready to live, they were "setting out": their train came to a stop in the middle of a field. They will go nowhere and they will do nothing. There sometimes comes back to them a confused memory of their magnificent turbulence. Then they wonder, "But what did we want?" And they don't remember. They have adjusted, but they suffer from chronic maladjustment. They will die of it. They are affluent bums: their bellies are full but they do nothing useful. I remember them as they were at twenty, so alive, so gay, so eager to relieve the old guard. I look at them today, with their faces ravaged by the cancer of surprise, and I think to myself, they didn't deserve that. As for the faithful vassals, some have not renewed their vows of fealty, others have sunk to a lower rank of vassalage. All are wretched. The first group have lost everything; they buzz about in dismay, hovering close to the ground like weightless mosquitos unable to alight. The others have sacrificed their organs of locomotion and taken root in the sand; they have become a form of vegetable life that the slightest puff of wind can change into a cloud of dust. Nomadic or sedentary, the same stupor unites them all. At what point, then, did their lives go astray? Nizan could tell them, both the desperate ones and the vassals. But I doubt that they are willing or able to read him. For a lost, tricked generation, this vigorous dead man tolls the knell.

But they have twenty-year-old sons, our grandsons, who have taken careful note of their defeats and ours. Until recently, prodigal sons told their fathers to go to hell and went over to the Left, bag and baggage. The rebel became a militant, it was classic. But what if their fathers are of the Left? What are they to do then? A young man came to see me. He loved his parents. "But," said he severely, "they're reactionaries." I have aged and words have aged with me: in my mind they are as old as I. I misunderstood. I took him for the scion of a wealthy family—good church members, liberals, perhaps, who voted for Pinay. He disabused me: "My father has been a Communist since the Congress of Tours." Another young man, the son of a Socialist, condemned both the SFIO* and the CP, saying "The Socialists are traitors and the Communists are fossils." And supposing the fathers were conservatives and supported Bidault? Is it likely that their sons would be attracted to the Left, that great, supine, worm-eaten corpse? It is stinking carrion. The powers of military men, dictatorship, and fascism are being born—or will be born—from its decomposition. It takes a strong stomach not to turn away from it in revulsion. We grandfathers were made by the Left. We lived by it; in it and by it we shall die. But we no longer have anything to say to the young men. Fifty years of life in this backward province that France has become is degrading. We have shouted, protested, signed, and counter-signed. According to our habits of thought, we have declared, "It is intolerable . . ." or, "The proletariat will never tolerate . . ." And in the end, we are still here—so we have accepted everything. Should we pass on to these unknown young men our wisdom and the fine fruits of our experience? In our progress from one abdication to another,

---

* Section Française de l'Internationale Ouvrière: the French Socialist party. (Trans.)

we have learned only one thing: our absolute impotence. I admit it. That is the beginning of Reason, of the fight for life. But our bones are old, and we are discovering that at the age when a young man plans to do something for posterity—we did nothing. Shall we tell the youth of today, "Be Cuban, be Russian or Chinese, whichever you prefer, be African?" They will reply that it's a little late to change their birth. In short, accountants or hoodlums, juvenile delinquents or trained technicians, they are struggling without hope and alone, against asphyxiation. Don't think that the ones who have chosen family and profession are resigned. They have only turned their violence inward and are destroying themselves. Their fathers have reduced them to impotence, and they cut off their own legs out of spite. The others break everything, strike anybody with anything—a knife, a bicycle chain. To escape their *malaise* they will blow up everything. But nothing blows up, and they find themselves at the police station, covered with blood. It was a fine Sunday; they'll do better next Sunday. To give blows or take them is all one to them, so long as blood flows. In the daze that follows a brawl, the only thing that hurts is their bruises, and they have the gloomy pleasure of not having to think.

Who will speak to these "angry young men"? Who can shed light on their violence? Nizan is their man. In his hibernation, he has grown younger year by year. Yesterday he was our contemporary, today he is theirs. When he was alive, we shared his rages. But in the end, not one of us performed "the simplest surrealist act,"* and now, here we are, grown old. We have betrayed our youth so often that it is only decent not to talk about it. Our old memories have lost their teeth and claws. Twenty years old? Yes, I must have been twenty once, but now I'm fifty-five, and I would not dare to write: "I was twenty. I will let no one say it is the best time of life." So much passion—and so lofty—from my pen would be demagoguery. Besides, I would

---

* "The simplest surrealist act is to go out into the street with a revolver in each hand and fire into the crowd at random as fast as you can." From André Breton's *Second Manifeste du Surréalisme* (1930). (Trans.)

be lying. The unhappiness of the young is total, I know that, maybe I felt it once, but it is still human, since it comes to them through men, their fathers or their older brothers. Ours comes from our arteries. We are strange objects, half eaten away by nature and vegetation, covered with ants; we are like tepid drinks, or the crazy paintings that amused Rimbaud. Young and violent, struck down by violent death, Nizan can step forward and speak to young people about youth: "I will let no one . . ." They will recognize their own voice. To those who keep their violence within themselves, he can say: "Your modesty will be the death of you, dare to desire, be insatiable, let loose the terrible forces that are warring and whirling inside you, do not be ashamed to ask for the moon—we must have it." And to the ones who vent their spleen at random: "Turn your rage against those who have provoked it, do not try to run away from your pain but seek out its causes and smash them." He can say anything to them because he is a young monster, a beautiful young monster like themselves, who shares their terror of dying and their hatred of living in the world we have made for them. He was alone, he became a Communist, ceased to be one, and died alone, near a window, on a staircase. This life can be explained by its intransigence: he became a revolutionary because he was a rebel, and when the revolution had to give way to the war, he found his violent youth again and finished as a rebel.

We both wanted to write. He published his first book long before I had written a word of mine. When *La Nausée* appeared, if we had valued these solemn introductions, it is he who would have written a preface for me. Death has reversed our roles. Death and systematic defamation. He will find his readers without my help—I have said who his natural public will be. But I thought this foreword was needed for two main reasons: to show the world how cunning and contemptible was the calumny devised against him, and to warn young men to give his words their full weight. They were young and hard, those words—it is we who have made them age. If I want to restore the brilliance that they had before the war, I must recall the wonderful time of

our refusals and make it live again, with Nizan, the man who said
"no" to the end. His death marked the end of a world. After him
the Revolution became constructive, the Left assented to everything, until one day in the fall of '58 it expired, murmuring a
final "yes." Let us try to recall the time of hatred, of unappeased
desire, of destruction—the time when André Breton, hardly
older than ourselves, wanted to see the Cossacks water their
horses in the fountains of the Place de la Concorde.

The error that I want my readers to avoid is one that I made
myself. And I made it during Nizan's lifetime, notwithstanding
the fact that we were such close friends that people used to
mistake us for each other. One day in June of '39, Léon
Brunschvicg ran into us at the offices of Gallimard and congratulated me on having written *Les Chiens de garde*, ". . . although," as he said without bitterness, "you were pretty hard on
me." I smiled at him in silence; Nizan stood smiling beside me.
The great idealist left without realizing his mistake. This confusion between us had been going on for eighteen years—it had
become our status in society, and we had come to accept it.
Particularly between 1920 and 1930, when we were students
together at the lycée and then the École Normale, we were
indistinguishable. Nevertheless, I did not see him as he really
was.

I could have drawn his portrait: medium height, black hair.
He had a cast in one eye, like me, but in the opposite direction,
so that it was agreeable. My divergent squint gave my face the
appearance of an unplowed field. His eyes converged, giving him
a mischievous air of abstraction even when he was listening. He
followed fashion closely, insolently. At seventeen he had his
pants cut so tight around the ankles that he had trouble pulling
them on. A little later they flared out into bell-bottoms that hid
his shoes. Then, all of a sudden, they changed into golf knickers
that came up to his knees and stood out like skirts. He carried a
Malacca walking stick and wore a monocle, little round collars,

and wing collars. He traded in his steel-rimmed glasses for enormous tortoise-shell spectacles which, with a touch of the English snobbery that afflicted all the young people of the time, he called his "goggles." I tried to emulate him, but my family organized an effective resistance and even went so far as to bribe the tailor. And besides, someone must have cast a spell over me: no sooner had I put them on than fine clothes changed into rags. I resigned myself to contemplating Nizan. With an amazement full of admiration. At the École Normale nobody paid any attention to dress except for a few provincials who proudly wore spats and tucked silk handkerchiefs into their jacket pockets. But I don't remember that anyone disapproved of Nizan's outfits —we were proud to have a dandy in our midst. He was attractive to women but kept them at a distance. To one who had come to our very room to offer herself to him, he replied, "Madame, we would soil ourselves." The truth was that he only liked young girls, and he chose the ones who were virgins and fools. He was fascinated by the dizzying secret of stupidity—the only real depth of mankind—and by the polished sheen of flesh without memories. Indeed, during the only affair I ever knew him to have, he was ceaselessly tormented by the vainest jealousy: he could not bear the thought that his mistress had a past. I found his conduct incomprehensible, although it was very clear. I obstinately insisted on regarding it as just another personality trait. I also took for personality traits his charming cynicism, his "black humor," his quiet, implacable aggressiveness. He never raised his voice, I never saw him frown or heard him speak harshly. He would bend his fingers over his palm and, as I said, become absorbed in the contemplation of his nails, loosing his violent words with a sly and deceptive serenity. Together we fell into all the traps. At sixteen he proposed that I become a superman, and I eagerly accepted. There would be the two of us. He was from Brittany and he gave us Gaelic names. We covered all the blackboards with these strange words: R'hâ and Bor'hou. He was R'hâ. One of our classmates wanted to share in our new-found dignity. We put him to the test. We demanded, for example, that he declare out loud, "I shit on the French army and the flag." These sentiments were not so daring as we imagined. They were current at the time and reflected the internationalism and anti-militarism of the old pre-war days. The candidate, however, shied away from them, and the two supermen remained alone and finally forgot all about being supermen. We used to spend hours, days, walking across Paris, discovering its flora and fauna, its stones, moved to tears at the sight of neon signs coming on. We thought that the world was new because we were new in the world. Paris was a bond between us, and we loved each other across the crowds of this gray city, under the lovely skies of its springtimes. We walked, we talked, we invented our own language, an intellectual slang such as all students make up. One night when they had nothing better to do, the supermen climbed the hill of the Sacré-Coeur and turning, saw spread out below them a profusion of glittering jewels. Nizan planted his cigarette in the left corner of his lips, twisted his mouth into a horrible grimace and said simply, "Hé! hé! Rastignac." I repeated, "Hé! hé!," as was fitting, and we walked down again, satisfied to have marked so discreetly the extent of our literary knowledge and the measure of our ambition. No one has written better about those walks, about that Paris, than my friend. One has only to reread *La Conspiration* to recapture the fresh, old-fashioned charm of that city that was the capital of the world and did not yet know it was to become a provincial backwater. The ambition, the quick changes of mood, the quiet white rages—I took it all as it came. That was the way Nizan was, calm and perfidious, charming. That was the way I loved him. He has described himself in *Antoine Bloyé* as "a taciturn adolescent, already plunged into the adventures of youth, leaving childhood behind him with a kind of avid exaltation." And that is the way I saw him. I learned about his taciturnity at my own expense. Once, while we were taking a preparatory course for the École Normale, we quarrelled and remained at odds with each other for six months. It was painful for me. At the École Normale, where we roomed together, there were times when he didn't speak to me for days. In our second year his mood grew even darker: he was going through a crisis whose outcome he could not foresee. He disappeared, and was found three days later, drunk, with strangers. And when our classmates questioned me about his "pranks," the only answer I could think of was that he was "in a rotten mood." He had told me, however, that he was afraid of dying. But since I was mad enough to think myself immortal, I criticized him and told him he was wrong: death was not worth a thought. Nizan's horror of death was like his retrospective jealousy—they were eccentricities that a healthy frame of mind should combat. When he couldn't stand it any longer, he left. He took a job as tutor with an English family in Aden. This departure scandalized the rest of us, rooted in the École as we were, but since Nizan intimidated us, we found a harmless explanation for it: love of travel. When he came back the following year, it was at night, and no one was expecting him. I was alone in my room. For an entire day I had been plunged in a state of pained indignation at the loose conduct of a young lady from the provinces. He entered without knocking. He looked pale, grim, a little out of breath. He said, "You don't look so cheery." "Neither do you," I replied. Whereupon we went off to have a drink and put the world on trial, delighted to have come to an understanding again. But it was only a misunderstanding: my anger was like a soap bubble, his was real. The horror of coming back to his cage and walking into it again, defeated, burned his throat. He was looking for help that no one could give him. His words of hate were pure gold, mine were counterfeit. The very next day he fled. He lived at his fiancée's, joined the CP, married, had a daughter, almost died of appendicitis, then, having passed his state examinations, got a job teaching philosophy at Bourg and ran for the legislature. I saw less of him. I was teaching in Le Havre, and then too, he led a family life—his wife had given him a second child, a son. But above all, the Party came between us. I was in sympathy with the Party, but I was not a member. I remained his boyhood friend, a petty bourgeois he was still fond of. Why didn't I understand him? There was no lack of signs. Why did I refuse to see them?

I think it was out of jealousy. I denied feelings I could not share. I sensed at once that he had incommunicable passions, a destiny that would separate us. I was afraid and I closed my eyes. At fifteen this son of a pious woman wanted to enter into Orders. I didn't know about it until a long time afterward. But I still remember how shocked and bewildered I was when he said to me one day as we strolled around the schoolyard at the lycée, "I had lunch at the minister's." He saw my stupefaction and explained with a detached air, "I might become converted to Protestantism." "You?," said I indignantly, "but . . . you don't believe in God." "No," he replied, "but their morality appeals to me." Madame Nizan threatened to cut off his allowance and the project was abandoned. But in that instant I had glimpsed behind this "piece of childishness" the impatience of a sick man who turns over and over in bed to escape his pain. I didn't want him to have this inaccessible pain—we had superficial melancholy in common and that was enough. For the rest, I tried to impose my optimism on him. I kept telling him that we were free. He would not answer, but the thin smile at the corner of his lips spoke volumes. At other times, he called himself a materialist—we were scarcely seventeen—and it was I who smiled disdainfully. Materialist, determinist: he felt the physical weight of his chains; I did not want to feel the weight of mine. I hated him to be involved in politics because I didn't feel the need of it myself. Communist, then royalist, then communist again, it was easy to mock him, and I did not deny myself the pleasure. In reality, his wide swings were the mark of his obstinacy. Nothing is more excusable at the age of eighteen than to hesitate between two opposite extremes. What never varied was his extremism. In any case, he was sure of one thing: the established order must be destroyed. For my part, I was pleased that this order existed so I could take pot shots at it with words. Nizan had a real need to unite with other men, so that together they might lift the stones that suffocated them. I wanted to think that this need was only the extravagance of a dandy. He was a communist in the same way that he wore a monocle, for the trifling pleasure of shocking people. He was unhappy at the École Normale, and I upbraided him for it: we were going to write, we would make beautiful books that would justify our existence. I didn't have anything to complain about, so why did he? In the middle of the second year, he suddenly announced that he was bored with literature and was going to become a cameraman. A friend gave him a few lessons. I was angry about it and when he explained that he had read so much and written so much that he had acquired a horror of words, and that he wanted to act directly on things, to transform them in silence, with his hands, he only made matters worse. He could not resign from the Word and condemn writing without passing judgment on me. It never occurred to me that Nizan, as we used to say, was seeking his salvation, and that "written cries" do not save.

He did not become a cameraman and I triumphed. But only briefly. His departure for Aden irritated me. For him it was a matter of life and death, and I guessed as much. To reassure myself, I decided it was another of his eccentricities. I had to admit that I counted for very little in his eyes, but today I ask myself, whose fault was that? Where could one find a more stubborn refusal to understand and, consequently, to help? When he came back from one of his binges, his panic-stricken flights, drunk and with death at his heels, I would welcome him tight-lipped and without a word, with all the dignity of an old wife who has resigned herself to outrages so long as it is understood she is keeping score. It's true he was hardly encouraging. He would go sit down at his table, somber, unkempt, his eyes bloodshot, and if I happened to speak to him he would look at me with blank hatred. No matter, it was my own fault that all I could think of was, "What a rotten disposition!" and that I never tried to understand these escapades, if only out of curiosity. His marriage I misunderstood completely. I was friendly with his wife, but celibacy was a moral principle with me, a rule of life. Therefore it could not be otherwise for Nizan. I decided that he had married Rirette because that was the only way he could have her. To tell the truth, I did not know that a young man who is in the grip of a terrible family can only free himself by starting a family of his own. I was born to be a bachelor all my days. I did not understand that celibacy weighed upon the bachelor living at my side, that he detested casual affairs—because they have a taste of death about them—just as he detested travel, and that when he said, "man is sedentary," or "give me my field . . . my needs, my men," he was simply asking for his share of happiness: a home, a wife, children.

When *Aden, Arabie* was published, I thought it was a good book and I was delighted. But I saw it only as a lively pamphlet, a whirlwind of light words. Many of his classmates made the same mistake—we were prejudiced. For most of us, including me, the first day at the École Normale was the beginning of independence. Many can say, as I do, that they had four years of happiness there. But here was a wild man who flew at our throats in a rage: "The École Normale . . . a ridiculous and, more often, odious thing, presided over by a patriotic, hypocritical, powerful little old man who respected the military." We were "adolescents worn out by years of lycée, corrupted by the humanities and by . . . bourgeois morality and bourgeois cooking." We decided to take it as a joke: "Say, he didn't think the place was such a dump when he was there, eh? I seem to remember the old boy had a pretty good time, with all us worn out adolescents." And we would start to recall our harmless pranks, remembering that he had gladly participated in them. Forgetting his flights, his scorn, the great rout that had swept him off to distant Arabia, we took his passion for mere extravagant rhetoric. As for me, I was foolishly hurt because he tarnished my memories. Since Nizan had shared my life at the École, he had to have been happy there, or else our friendship was already dead at that time. I preferred to save the past. I said to myself, "He's exaggerating." Today I think our friendship was indeed already dead, through no fault of ours, and that Nizan, consumed with loneliness, needed to go and fight in the midst of men rather than to bandy words with an unfaithful and all too familiar reflection of himself. It was I who maintained our friendship and embalmed it, by deliberately shutting my eyes, by lying. The truth is that our paths had separated and we were steadily drawing apart. Many years have had to pass, and I have had to understand my own path at last, before I could speak with certainty about his.

The more sinister life is, the more absurd is death. I do not deny that a man in the midst of work, in the fullness of hope, can be struck, as by a flash of lightning, by the sudden realization of death. I do say that a young man is afraid of death when he is dissatisfied with life. Before he is led by the hand to the seat that awaits him, a student is something infinite, undefined. He moves easily from one doctrine to another, held by none, finding all systems of thought equivalent. In reality, what we call teaching the "humanities" in school is only teaching the great errors of the past. Molded by our Republics in the image of Valéry's Monsieur Teste—that ideal citizen who never says anything or does anything but who knows what the score is all the same— these young men will take twenty years to understand that ideas are stones, that they have an inflexible order, and that they must be used for building. As long as worn out men, discreet to the point of being transparent, push bourgeois objectivity so far that they ask their students to see things from Nero's point of view, then Loyola's, then Monsieur Thiers', each of these apprentices is going to think he is pure Mind, that colorless, tasteless gas that sometimes expands to the galaxies and sometimes condenses into formulas. The young élite are everything and nothing: in other words, they are supported by the state and by their families. Underneath this misty indistinctness their life burns away. Suddenly pure Mind is brought up short against death. In vain does it try to encompass and dissolve it: death is unthinkable. An accident strikes a body, a brute fact is going to terminate the brilliant indetermination of ideas. This shocking realization awakens more than one terrified adolescent at night. Universal Culture is no recourse against capital punishment and its incomprehensible singularity. Later, when the individuality of his body is reflected in the individuality of the work he has undertaken, a young man integrates his death with his life and sees it as just one more risk along with all the others that threaten his work and his family. For those few men who are lucky enough to love what they do, the final shipwreck, which grows less terrifying the nearer it comes, is converted into the small change of day-to-day concerns.

I have described the fate common to us all. That is nothing. But when the terror of death outlasts adolescence, when it becomes the profound secret of the adult and the mainspring of his decisions, the sick man understands his affliction: his terror of soon ceasing to live simply reflects his horror at still having to live. Death is the irrevocable sentence. It condemns the wretched, for all eternity, to have been only that: shameful calamities. Nizan dreaded that fate. He was a monster crawling blindly among all the other monsters, afraid that one day he would explode and there would be nothing left of him. When he put the following words in the mouth of one of his characters, he had known for a long time that death was the definitive illumination of life: "If I think about my death, it's for good reason. My life is hollow and death is all it deserves." In the same book, Bloyé comes to fear "the uniform visage of his life . . . and [this fear] rises from a yet deeper region of the body than the bleeding places where the warning signs of disease are formed."

What, in sum, was the cause of his suffering? Why did I, more than all others, sound ridiculous to him when I talked about our liberty? If he believed, from the time he was sixteen, in the inexorable chain of causes, it was because he felt constrained and manipulated: "We have within us divisions, alienations, wars, debates. . . . Each of us is divided among the men he might be. . . ." A solitary child, he was too conscious of his uniqueness to throw himself into universal ideas, the way I did. A slave, he came to philosophy to free himself, and Spinoza furnished him a model. In the first two types of knowledge, man remains a slave because he is incomplete; knowledge of the third type breaks down the partitions, the negative determinants. It is all one, according to this mode, to return to the infinite substance and to achieve the affirmative totality of one's particular essence.

Nizan wanted to pull down all walls: he would unify his life by proclaiming his desires and subduing them.

The most evident desire springs from sex and its frustrated appetites. In a society that reserves its women for the old and the rich, this desire is the first misfortune of a poor young man and a foretaste of the troubles that lie ahead. Nizan spoke bitterly about the old men who slept with our women and wanted to castrate us. But to tell the truth, we were living in the age of the Great Desire. The surrealists wanted to arouse that infinite concupiscence whose object is nothing less than Everything. Nizan sought a remedy and took what he could find. Through the works of the surrealists he discovered Freud and placed him in his Pantheon. As revised and corrected by Breton and by a young writer in danger, Freud resembled Spinoza: he tore away the veils and cobwebs, he imposed harmony on the enemies that slaughtered each other in our tunnels, dissolved in light the deformed monsters raging inside us, and reduced us to the unity of powerful appetites. My friend tried him for a while, not without some success. We find traces of this influence even in *Antoine Bloyé*, in this fine sentence, for example: "As long as men are not complete and free, they will dream at night." Antoine dreams, about the women he has not had, has not even dared long for. On awaking, he refuses to heed "this voice of wisdom" because "he who wakes and he who sleeps rarely understand one another." Antoine is an old man, but here Nizan speaks from experience, I know. He used to dream, he dreamed until the day of his death. His letters from the front are filled with his dreams.

But it was only a working hypothesis, a provisional means of achieving unity. He worshipped women who passed him on the street, pale forms that faded in the light and smoke of Paris, fleeting symbols of love. But he loved them best when they were inaccessible. This serious, literary young man intoxicated himself with privations—that can be useful to a writer. But let no one suppose that chastity weighed heavily on him: one or two affairs—short and painful—and the rest of the time, shining young girls whom he touched lightly as they slipped past. He would have been only too happy to find in himself simply a conflict between the flesh and the law. He would have judged between them and condemned the law. "Morality is an asshole," he used to say at twenty.* In fact, the taboos are more insidious, and we ourselves are their accomplices. Morality never came out in the open, but in the presence of all women except virgins, his agitation was accompanied by a feeling of revulsion. Later on, when he had his "field" and his "men," I heard him marvel over the beauty of the *whole* female body, praising it in utter amazement, but precisely.

At the time I wondered what had prevented him from making so widespread a discovery when he was involved in his devastating love affairs. Now I know: it was disgust, an infantile repugnance for bodies he thought were worn out by former caresses. As adolescents, when we looked at women I wanted all of them; he wanted only one, and one who would be his. He could not conceive that it was possible to love unless one loved from morning till night, or that there could be possession when one did not possess the woman, when she did not possess you. He thought that man is sedentary, that casual affairs are like travel— abstractions. A thousand and three women are a thousand and three times the same, and he wanted one woman who would be a thousand and three times another. He would love in her, as a promise against death, even the secret signs of fecundity.

In other words, the frustration of the senses was an effect, not a cause. When he married it disappeared. The Great Desire fell back into place and became just one more need like all the others that one satisfies incompletely, too quickly, or not at all. In fact, Nizan suffered from his present contradictions only to interpret them in the light of the future. If he tried to kill himself one day, it was to put an end at once to what he believed was only a beginning all over again. He was marked from childhood by Breton piety—too much or too little for his happiness. Contra-

---

* A remark that is rather humorous in the original because it rhymes: "*Morale, c'est trou de balle.*" (Trans.)

diction had been installed under his roof. He was the child of an old couple, two adversaries who had begotten him during a truce and, when he was born, resumed their quarrel. His father, who had been first a railroad worker then an engineer, set him the example of a way of thinking that was technical, unbelieving and adult, and revealed in his conversation a sad loyalty to the class he had left. From earliest childhood, Nizan internalized this mute conflict between an old and childish woman of the bourgeoisie and a renegade member of the working class. It became the foundation for his future personality. No matter how young he is, the child of a charwoman participates in his family's future: the father makes plans. But the Nizans had no future. Monsieur Nizan was general foreman of a railroad yard, almost at the height of his career. What had he to look forward to? A promotion due him, a few honors, retirement and death. Madame Nizan lived simultaneously in the critical moment when the onions must be browned or the cutlet seared, and that fixed moment called Eternity. The child was not far from the place where he had started, nor the family from its ultimate destination. Dragged down in his parents' decline, he wanted to learn, to build, and everything was disintegrating before his eyes, even the conjugal quarrel. It had long since changed into indifference; it now existed only inside him. In the silence, he heard his parents' dialogue: the trifling, ceremonious prattle of Faith was occasionally interrupted by a harsh voice which gave a name to plants, stones, and tools. These two voices warred with each other. At first the pious talk seemed to be winning out; his mother spoke about Charity, about Paradise, and the Supreme End, and all that eschatology challenged the precise activity of the technicians. What was the point in making locomotives? There were no trains to heaven. The engineer used to leave the house as soon as he could. Between the ages of five and ten, his son would follow him into the fields, take his hand, and run along beside him. At twenty-five, he had fond memories of these walks for men only, that were so obviously directed against the wife and mother. I should note, however, that he preferred not the sciences, but the weary courtesy of the Word. When a worker becomes an engineer and suffers from the gaps in his education, the classic thing is for him to send his son to the École Polytechnique. But Nizan showed a suspicious dislike for mathematics. He studied Greek and Latin instead. I was the step-son of a graduate of Polytechnique, but I too disliked the sciences, for different reasons. We both loved vague, ritualistic words, and myths. But his father had his revenge. Under the influence of his positivism, my friend tried to break away from the glass trinkets of religion. I have already mentioned the stages of this deliverance: the mystical transport—Catholicism's last gasp—that almost led him to take Orders, his flirtation with Calvin, the metamorphosis of his devout Catharism into political Manichaeism, royalism, and finally Marxism. For a long time he and I retained the Christian vocabulary. We were atheists who never doubted we had been put on earth to find our salvation there and, with a little luck, the salvation of others. There was only one difference between us: I was certain that I was of the elect, Nizan often wondered if he was not damned. From his mother and from Catholicism he got his utter contempt for the works of this world, the fear of succumbing to worldly temptations, and the taste—which he never lost—for pursuing an absolute End. He had been persuaded that hidden within him, under the tangle of day-to-day concerns, was a beautiful totality, white and flawless. He had to burn the brush and uproot the weeds—then the indivisible Eternity would manifest itself in all its purity. Accordingly, at this time he judged his father's job to be obsessive and pointless activity: primary ends were being sacrificed to means, man to the machine. He soon ceased to believe in the little white pills of life called souls; yet he retained the obscure feeling that his father had lost his.

These ancient superstitions do not prevent a man from living, *if he has Faith*. But technique, disqualified, took its revenge by wringing the neck of religion. Nizan was still dissatisfied, but his dissatisfactions were now uprooted and afloat. Worldly activities may be a farce, but if nothing exists except the earth and the human creatures that scratch it, the children of men must take the next shift and set to scratching too. There can be no other occupation, unless one falsifies the ancient Christian words. When Nizan made the strange proposal that we be supermen, it was not so much out of pride as from an obscure need to escape our condition. Alas! it only meant changing names. From that time until he left for Aden, he never stopped dragging his chains, or forging symbols of escape.

But it is impossible to understand Nizan's anguish unless one recalls what I said earlier: he interpreted the present, which for him was laborious, disenchanted, broken only by brief periods of exaltation, in the sinister light of a future that was really his father's past. "I was afraid. My departure was the child of fear." Fear of what? He says it in this book: "Mutilations . . . awaited us. After all, we knew how our parents lived." He has developed this sentence in a long and beautiful novel, *Antoine Bloyé*. In it he recounts the life and death of his father. And although Nizan hardly appears in the book, he continually speaks of himself. First, he is the witness of his father's decay. Second, since his father confided in no one, we know that all the thoughts and feelings attributed to him have been torn from the author's heart and projected onto the distraught old man. This constant dual presence is a sign of what the analysts call identification with the father.

I have said that in his early years Nizan admired his father. He envied his strength, which was sterile but visible, his silences, his hands that had toiled. Monsieur Nizan used to talk about his former comrades, and fascinated by these men who knew the truth about life and who apparently loved each other, the little boy saw his father as a worker and wanted to be like him in everything. He would have his father's earthly patience. It would take nothing less than the obscure inner density of things, of matter, to save the future monk from his mother, from *Monsieur le Curé,* and from his own idle chatter. "Antoine," he said admiringly, "was a corporal man. His mind was not so pure that it took no interest in the body which nourished it and which for so many years had provided it with an admirable proof of existence."

But the admirable man staggered. All of a sudden the child saw him start to disintegrate. Nizan had given himself to his father without reservation: "I will be like him." Now he had to watch the interminable decomposition of his own future: "That will be me." His mother's prattle triumphed. He saw Matter sink beneath the waves, while the Soul remained afloat like foam after a shipwreck. What happened? Nizan tells the story in *Antoine Bloyé*. For reasons which I do not know—because while he stayed fairly close to the truth in his book, he doubtless changed the circumstances—the man on whom he modeled Antoine tried to draw up a balance sheet when he was only forty. Everything had begun with that false victory he had won—the crossing of a line—at a time when the bourgeoisie was promising everyone "the great future of equal opportunity," a time when "every workingman's son carried in his school bag . . . a bourgeois' diploma with the name left blank." By the time he was fifteen his life was already like the express trains he would later run, trains that were "borne along by a force full of certainty and suffocation." And then, in 1883, he was graduated from the École des Arts et Métiers, eighteenth out of a class of seventy-seven. Shortly thereafter, at the age of twenty-seven, he married Anne Guyader, the daughter of his general foreman. From that time on, "everything was settled, established. There was no appeal." He sensed this at the very moment when the curé united them, and then he forgot his misgivings. The years passed, the couple went from one city to another, constantly moving in and moving out, never settling anywhere. Time wore on, and life remained provisional. Every day, in its abstraction, was like every other day. Antoine dreamed, without too much conviction, that "something would happen." Nothing happened. He consoled himself with the thought that he would show what stuff he was made of when real battles came along. But while he waited for great circumstances, the little ones rubbed against him and imperceptibly wore him down. "True courage consists of overcoming small enemies." Nevertheless he advanced irresistibly. At first, listening to the bourgeois sirens, he experienced "the most insidious peace." By fulfilling the false duties set before him—duties toward the Company, toward Society, *even* toward his former comrades—he achieved what might be called a vital minimum of good conscience. But "the years piled up," the desires, hopes, and memories of youth sank into that shadowy realm of condemned thoughts where human forces founder. The Company devoured its agents. For fifteen years there was no more selfless man than Antoine Bloyé, driven by "the demands, the ideas, the judgments of his work." He hardly ran his eye over the newspapers: "the events they recounted were taking place on another planet and did not concern him." But he was fascinated by "descriptions of machines" in technical journals. He lived, or rather his body imitated the attitudes of life. But in reality the mainspring of his life, the motives for his acts, did not lie within him. "Complicated powers prevented him from planting his feet firmly on the earth." One could apply to him, with hardly a change of words, what Nizan writes about a rich Englishman in Aden: "Each of us is divided among the men he might be, and Mr. C. has allowed to triumph within him that man for whom life consists of making the price of . . . Abyssinian leather go up or down. . . . Fighting abstract entities such as firms, unions, merchants' guilds—are you going to call that action?" Of course Bloyé did not have so much power as the Englishman, but what of that? Was not everything in his job abstract: plans, estimates, red tape? Was not everything already decided somewhere else, very far away, by other men? The man had become an extension of his company, and his total immersion in his work still left a vital part of him unused. He slept little, never spared himself, carried sacks and beams on his back, and was always the last to leave his office, but as Nizan says, "all his work concealed the fact that he was essentially idle." I know. I spent ten years of my life under the thumb of a graduate of the École Polytechnique. He killed himself on the job—or rather, somewhere, in Paris no doubt, the job had decided that it would kill him. He was the most insignificant of men. On Sunday he would withdraw into himself, find a desert there, and lose himself in it. He held on, though, saved by his sluggishness or his rages of wounded vanity. Fortunately, it was war time when they retired him. He read the papers, clipped articles and pasted them into a notebook. At least he made no pretense: his flesh was abstract. But for Bloyé's young son, there was the shock of an unbearable contradiction. Antoine had a real body that was tough and capable and had once been avid, and that body imitated life. And yet, set in motion by distant abstractions, he had scuttled his rich passions and voluntarily transformed himself into an abstraction. "Antoine was a man who had a profession and a temperament, that was all. That is all a man is, in the world in which Antoine Bloyé lived. There are nervous merchants, full-blooded engineers, bilious workers, choleric notaries. People say those things and think they have made an effort to define a man. They also say a black dog, a striped cat. A doctor . . . had told him, 'You, you're the nervous, full-blooded type.' There. That said everything. Everyone could handle him, like a coin whose value is known. He circulated among other coins."

The boy worshipped his father, and I do not know if he would have noticed this inner poverty by himself. Nizan's misfortune lay in the fact that his father was better than the next man. After having ignored many danger signs, Monsieur Nizan finally realized what he was, too late, and came to have a horror of his life. He saw his death and loathed it. For nearly half a century he had practiced self-deception, trying to believe that he could still "become a new man, a different man who would be truly himself." Suddenly he realized that it was impossible for him to change. This impossibility was death at the heart of life. Death draws a line and adds up the sum, but for Nizan's father the line was already drawn and the sum added. This schematic creature, who was as much a generalization as an individual, shared the bed of a woman who was no more a particular person than was he, but rather a broadcasting station for the dissemination of pious thoughts manufactured in Rome, and who, like himself, had doubtless repressed simple and voracious needs. He proclaimed their double failure to his frightened son. He would get up at night, "throw his clothes over his arm, and dress at the foot of the stairs. . . . He would go out. . . . 'I'm a fifth wheel,' he would say to himself, 'I am superfluous, I serve no purpose, I have already ceased to exist, if I let myself fall into the water no one would notice it, there would just be the announcements edged in black. I'm a failure, I'm finished. . . .' He would turn back toward the house . . . shivering, pass his hand over his face and feel that his beard had grown during the night. Near the house his awakened wife and son would be looking for him, calling him. He would hear their shrill voices from afar but would not answer, leaving them in anxiety until the last minute, as if to punish them. They were afraid he might have killed himself. . . . When he came up to them, he would say with stifled anger, 'So I can't do as I please any more . . . ?' And he would go back up to his room without paying any further attention to them."

These nocturnal flights are not an invention of the novelist. Nizan used to talk to me about his father, and I know that it is all true. Meditation on death drives a man toward suicide—it makes him dizzy and impatient. I ask you to imagine the feelings of an adolescent whose mother wakes him up at night saying, "Your father is not in his room. This time I'm sure he's going to kill himself." Death enters into him, death takes up its stand at the crossroads of all his routes; it is the end and the beginning. His father was already dead and wanted to go before he was summoned. That is the meaning and the conclusion of a stolen life. But his father's life occupied Nizan like a foreign power. His father infected him with the death which was to come. When this disenchanted old man—the doctors said neurasthenic —fled the house, driven by fear, his son dreaded two deaths in one: the first, in its imminence, foreshadowed the other and gave it the face of terror. The father bayed at death, and every night the child died of fright. In this return to nothingness of a life that was nothing, the child thought he saw his own destiny.

Henceforth "everything was settled, established. There was no appeal." He would be this superfluous young man, then this carcass, then nothing. He had identified with the strong maturity of another man, and when that man revealed his mortal weakness, my friend alienated himself from it. The engineer's unseemly wandering became more frequent when Nizan turned fifteen. And it was between fifteen and sixteen that the adolescent took out insurance on eternal life: in a final effort, he asked the Church for immortality. Too late. Once faith is lost, a feeling of disgust for the world is not enough to bring it back. He lived his alienation. He thought he was another man and interpreted each moment in the light of another existence. Everywhere he came upon the same traps that had been set for his father: affable, deceitful people tried to get around him with flattery or false victories—academic honors, small gifts, invitations. The engineer's son would enter the teaching profession. And what then? Teachers, like general foremen, move into houses and out of them, run through towns, marry the daughters of the petty bourgeoisie of the provinces, and out of self-interest or weakness, align themselves on the side of their masters. Are they any the less divided than the technicians? And which is better? To make locomotives to serve a few great lords of the bourgeois state, or to give children a foretaste of death by teaching them dead languages, fake history and a lying morality? Do university professors show more indulgence "for their great sorrows, for the adventures lying coiled in the chinks of their bodies?" All these petty bourgeois are of the same species. An imbecilic dignity is imposed on them, they castrate themselves, the real purpose of their work escapes them, and they wake up at fifty just in time to watch themselves die.

From the time we were sixteen I thought we were united by the same desire to write. I was mistaken. A clumsy hunter, I was dazzled by words because I always missed them. Nizan was more precocious and his gamebag was full. He discovered words everywhere, in dictionaries, in books, and even at large, on people's lips. I admired his vocabulary, and the ease with which he worked newly acquired words into his rough drafts—words like "bimetalism" and "percolator." But he was far from being totally committed to literature. I was in it up to my ears, the discovery of an adjective enchanted me. As for him, he wrote better than I did and watched himself write—with the mournful eyes of his father. Words burst apart or withered into dead leaves: can one justify oneself by words? In the face of death, literature became a parlor game, a variation on canasta. It is only natural for a professor to write, he is encouraged to do so. The same traps serve for the writer as for the engineer: flattery, temptations. At the age of forty all these lackeys will be carcasses. Honors hid Valéry. He lived off princes, queens, and powerful industrialists. He dined at their table because he worked for them. The glorification of the Word is of direct profit to the high and mighty: it teaches men to take the word for the thing, and that is cheaper. Nizan understood that. He was afraid of wasting his life collecting the breath of voices.

He started to *repeat* the somber follies of his father. He too began the midnight excursions, the flights. He would walk the streets and suddenly "he would sense that he was going to die, and all at once he would become a man apart from all the passers-by. . . . He knew this thing by a single act of perception, with a particular and perfect knowledge." It was not an idea but "a completely naked terror . . . that disdained all forms." At such times he thought he was in possession of a fundamental, material intuition, that he was learning about the indivisible unity of his body from the unity of its absolute negation. I think he was entirely mistaken: we do not have even that, not even a direct communication with our nothingness. In reality a shock had awakened the old, familiar anguish: in him, his father's life was slipping away, and the eye of the *other* death opened again, draining the color from his modest pleasures. The street became a hell.

At such moments he hated us. "The friends he met, the women he glimpsed were life's accomplices, and they were drawing checks against time." He would never have dreamed of asking us for help. We had no awareness, we would not even have understood him: "Which of these madmen loved him shrewdly enough to protect him from death." He fled our rapacious countenances, our eager mouths, our greedy nostrils, our eyes always fixed on the future. Missing. Three days of suicide, winding up with a hangover. He *reproduced* his father's nocturnal crises. They grew in magnitude and ended up in drink and more words. I think he overdid the tragedy of it all, since he could not attain the perfect, grim sincerity of a man of fifty. Never mind—his anguish did not lie. And if anyone wants to know the most profound and individual truth about him, I would say it was *that* and nothing else: the death agony of an old man gnawing at the life of a very young one. He had fire and passion, and then that implacable stare froze everything. In order to judge himself from day to day, Nizan had placed himself on the other side of the grave. Actually, he was going around in circles. There was the haste to live, the terror of arriving at the end, the time that was wearing away, the "years piling up," the pitfalls he barely escaped, the man-hunt whose meaning he did not completely understand. Yet in spite of it all, there were also his muscles and his blood: how can you prevent a well fed young bourgeois from having confidence in the future? He would sometimes experience a somber enthusiasm, but his own exaltation frightened him and aroused mistrust: supposing it were a trap, one of those lies that one tells oneself to smother terror and suffering? The only thing he loved in himself was his revolt. It proved that he was still resisting, that he had not yet entered upon those rails that lead irresistibly to the siding. But when he thought about his revolt he was afraid it would weaken: they threw so many blankets over me that they almost had me. They'll try it again. Supposing I just quietly got used to the life they have all laid out for me. Around the years 1925-1926, he had a wild terror of becoming accustomed. "So many bonds to break, secret timidities to overcome, small battles to fight. . . . One is afraid of being . . . unbearably unique, of no longer being like everybody else . . . false courage awaits great occasions;

true courage consists of overcoming small enemies every day."
Would he finally be able to overcome these gnawing enemies?
In five or ten years would he still be able to break all these
bonds, which were growing more numerous every day? He was
living in enemy territory, surrounded by the familiar signs of
universal alienation: "just try, while still in your arrondissements
and sub-prefectures, to forget your civic and filial obligations . . ."
Everything tempted him to sleep, to give up, to resign himself.
He had reached the point of counting up his abdications, "the
terrible old habits." He was also afraid of that alibi dear to men
of culture: the vain noise in his head, of torn and precious words.
In reality, meditation on death has other consequences, graver
than intermittent conversations: it disenchants. I ran after
sparks that for him were only ashes. He wrote, "I tell you that
all men are bored." Now the worst consequence of boredom, that
"continual forewarning of death," is that for sensitive souls it
produces a by-product: the inner life. Nizan was afraid that in
the end, his very real disgust would give him an over-refined
subjectivity, and that he would lull his grievances to sleep to
the purring of "sham thoughts, of ideas that are . not really
ideas." These aborted offspring of our impotence distract our
attention from our bleeding sores. We must never sleep. But
Nizan, with his eyes wide open, felt sleep mounting in him.

This revolt is an example to the sons of the bourgeoisie, because it is not the direct result of hunger or exploitation. Nizan
sees every life through the cold windowpane of death. In his
eyes, each one becomes a balance sheet. His fundamental alienation sharpens his perceptions and enables him to ferret out all
kinds of alienation. With what gravity he interrogates us, like a
believer, in the presence of our death: "What didst thou do
with thy youth?" What a profound and sincere desire to knit up
the scattered strands in each of us, to contain our disorders in the
synthetic unity of a form: "Will man never be anything but a
fragment of man, alienated, mutilated, a stranger to himself?
How many parts of man left uncultivated, how many things in
him aborted!"

This cry of protest by a "sub-man" forms the hollow outline of the real man he wanted to be. He set aside his mystical transports, his taste for adventure, his word castles. The inaccessible image remained simple and familiar: man would be a free and harmonious body. There is a wisdom of the body, always stifled, always present since Adam—"in the darkest region of our being are hidden our most authentic needs." It is not a question of being madly in love, or of undertaking tasks that are beyond us. Man is sedentary, he loves the earth because he can touch it, he enjoys producing life. The Great Desire was only an empty phrase. There remain *desires*, which are modest but concrete, and which balance one another. Nizan was drawn to Epicurus and wrote very well about him later: *there* was a man who addressed himself to everyone, including prostitutes and slaves, and never lied to them.

One is reminded of Rousseau, and not without cause. City dweller though he was, Nizan was faithful to his childhood in that he retained a kind of rustic naturalism. One may wonder how this noble savage would have adapted to the necessities of socialist production and interplanetary travel. It is true: the only way for us to regain the freedom we have lost is to invent it. It is forbidden to turn back, even if only to take stock of our "authentic" needs.

But let us leave epicureanism and Rousseau. These are only fleeting suggestions, and I do not want to push them too far. Like all petty bourgeois of his time, Nizan began with individualism. He wanted to be *himself*, and the whole world separated him from himself. Against the abstractions, against the symbolic entities they were trying to slip into his heart and muscles, he was defending his own particular life. He never wasted time describing the plenitude of moments or passions— that does not exist. That is what they rob us of. Instead, he said that love is real and that we are prevented from loving; that life could be real, that it could bring forth a real death, but that we are made to die before we are even born. He showed that in this world where everything is upside down, where the final defeat is the truth of a life, we have many "encounters with death," and each time, confused signs awaken "our most authentic needs." Antoine and Anne Bloyé have a little girl. She is doomed and they know it. Grief draws together these abstract figures who have been living in solitude in the midst of their promiscuity. But only for a little while. Individuals can never be saved by the singularity of an accident.

By the time Nizan was fifteen he had understood the essentials. That was because of the nature of his malady. It is true that certain alienations are all the more dangerous because they hide behind an abstract feeling of freedom. But Nizan never felt free: he had been *possessed*. The "awkward misery" of his father occupied him like an external power, forced itself upon him, imposed a dictatorship, destroyed his pleasures and his bursts of enthusiasm. And you could not even say that this wretched destiny had come from the former workingman. It came from every horizon, from all of France, from Paris. Nizan had tried for a while—at the time of his mysticism, of R'hâ and Bor'hou— to struggle alone, and to overcome the disgust and discord within him by means of words and religious exaltation. But the structure of society crushes us. Spinoza came to his assistance: we must act upon causes. But supposing the causes are not in our hands? He tried to analyze his experience: "What man can triumph over his division? He cannot triumph alone, because the causes of that division lie outside himself." It was time to bid a contemptuous farewell to spiritual exercises. "I was under the impression that human life could be discovered through revelation: what mysticism." It was obvious that he must fight, and that he could do nothing alone. Since everything came from elsewhere, even the contradictions that had produced his most personal character traits, it was elsewhere and everywhere that the battle would be waged. Others would fight for him *out there; here* Nizan would fight for others. The only problem for the moment was to see clearly, to recognize his brothers in shadow.

As early as his second year at the École Normale he had been drawn to the Communists. In short, he had come to a conclusion. But decisions are made in the dark, and without realizing it, we struggle for a long time against our own will. He had to knock on every door, try everything, experiment with solutions he had long since rejected. I think he wanted to experience the good things of this world before he took the vow of poverty. He departed for Aden to have a last fling. And then fear welled up in him: he had to break off. Aden was his last temptation, his last attempt to find an individual solution. His last flight too: Arabia beckoned to him the way on certain evenings the Seine had beckoned to his father. Did he not later write of Antoine Bloyé that he "would have liked to abandon this existence . . . to become a new man, a different man who would be truly himself. He imagined himself . . . lost, like a man who has left no address, a man who does things, who breathes." He had to flee us and flee himself.

We lost him; he never lost himself. He was tormented by a new abstraction: to run from one place to another, from one woman to another, is to hold on to nothing. Aden was Europe compressed, and at white heat. One day Nizan did what his father, who was still living, had never dared to do. He took an open car and set out at high noon without a sun helmet. They found him in a ditch, unconscious but unhurt. This suicide liquidated a few of the old terrors. When he recovered, he looked around him and saw "the most naked state, the economic state." Colonies expose a regime which, in the metropolitan countries, is shrouded in mists. He came back. He had understood the causes of our servitude. His terror became an aggressive force: hate. He was no longer fighting against insidious, anonymous infiltrations. He had seen naked exploitation and oppression, and he had understood that his adversaries had names and faces, that they were men. Miserable, alienated men, doubtless, like his father and himself. But men who "defended and preserved their misery and its causes, with guile, with violence, with obstinacy and skill." That night when he came back and knocked at my door, he knew that he had tried everything, that his back was to the wall, that all solutions were blind alleys except one:

war. He was coming back among his enemies to fight: "I will no longer be afraid to hate. I will no longer be ashamed to be fanatic. I owe them the worst: they all but destroyed me."

The end. He found his community and was received into it; it protected him against his enemies. But since I am introducing him to the young readers of today, I must answer the question they will not fail to ask: Did he finally find what he was looking for? What could the Party give to this man who had been skinned alive, who suffered to the very marrow of his bones from the sickness of death? We must be scrupulous about asking this question. I am telling the story of an exemplary life, which is just the opposite of an edifying life. Nizan shed his skin, and yet the old man, the old young man, remained. From 1929 to 1939 I saw less of him, but our meetings were all the more lively for being brief, and they taught me much about him. Nowadays, I understand, one chooses the family as opposed to politics. Nizan, however, had chosen both. Aeneas had grown weary of carrying gloomy old Anchises for so long, and with one shrug of the shoulders had sent him sprawling. Nizan had rushed into marriage and fatherhood in order to kill his father. But becoming a father is not in itself a sufficient cure for childhood. On the contrary, the authority vested in the new head of a family condemns him to repeat the age-old pieces of childishness handed down to us from Adam through our parents. It was an old story to my friend. He wanted to finish off once and for all the father who in each generation was murdered by his son only to be reborn again in him. He would become a *different* man, and would keep himself from capricious behavior in the family by public discipline. Let us see if he succeeded.

The doctrine satisfied him completely. He detested conciliations and conciliators, and most especially their Great Master, Leibnitz. When he was required to study the *Discourse on Metaphysics* in school, he took his revenge by making a talented drawing of the philosopher in full flight, wearing a Tyrolean hat, with the imprint of Spinoza's boot on his right buttock. To pass from the *Ethics* to *Das Kapital*, however, was easy. Marxism became his second nature or, if you prefer, his Reason. His eyes were Marxist, and his ears. And his head. At last he understood his incomprehensible wretchedness, his wants, his terror. He saw the world and saw himself in it. But above all, at the same time that Marxism made his hatreds legitimate, it reconciled in him the opposing discourse of his parents. The rigor of technique, the exactitude of science, the patience of reason, all that was retained. But the doctrine also went beyond the pettiness of positivism, with its absurd refusal to "know through causes." The dreary world of means, and of the means of means, was left to the engineers. To the troubled young man who wanted to save his soul, Marxism offered absolute ends: play midwife to history, bring forth the revolution, prepare Man and the Reign of Man. The doctrine did not concern itself with salvation or personal immortality, but it gave him the chance to live on, anonymously or gloriously, in the midst of a common enterprise that would end only with the species. He put everything into Marxism: physics and metaphysics, his passion for action and his passion for retrieving his acts, his cynicism and his eschatological dreams. Man was his future. But now was the time to slash. It would be up to other men to sew the pieces together again. His was the pleasure of cheerfully ripping everything to shreds for the good of humanity.

Everything suddenly took on weight, even words. He distrusted words because they served bad masters, but everything changed when he was able to turn them against the enemy. He used their ambiguity to confuse, their vague charm to beguile. In the service of the Party, literature could even become idle chitchat. The writer, like the ancient sage, could turn a triple somersault if he wanted to. All the words belonged to the enemies of man; the Revolution gave permission to steal them, that was all. That was enough. For ten years Nizan had been plundering, and all of a sudden he brought forth the sum total of his thefts: vocabulary. He understood his role as a communist writer, and he understood that it was the same thing for him to discredit the enemies of man and to discredit their language. No holds barred—the law of the jungle. The Word of the masters is a lie. Not only will we pick their sophisms apart, but we will invent sophisms to use against them, we will lie to them. We will even indulge in farce, to prove by our speech that the speech of the Master is a farce. Today these games have become suspect. The East is in a constructive stage; it has given us in the provinces a new respect for "bibelots of sonorous inanity."* I have said that we were serious—caught between two counterfeit currencies, one of which comes from the East, the other from the West. In 1930 there was only one, and in France the Revolution was only in the destructive stage.

The mission of the intellectual was to muddle the words and tangle the threads of bourgeois ideology. Snipers were setting fire to the brush and whole linguistic sectors were being reduced to ashes. Nizan rarely played the clown and did not go in much for sleight of hand. He lied, as we all did in that golden age, when he was very sure that no one would believe him. Calumny had just been born. It was nimble and gay and had a touch of poetry about it. But these practices reassured him. We know that he wanted to write—against death—and that death had changed the words into dead leaves under his pen. He had been afraid of being duped, afraid of wasting his life playing with wind. Now he was told that he had not been mistaken, that literature was a weapon in the hands of our masters. He was given a new mission: in a negative period, a book can be an act, if the revolutionary writer makes it his business to change the conditions of language. He could do anything he wanted, even create his own style. For the wicked, it would be the sugar-coating on the bitter pill; for the good, a call to vigilance—when the sea sings, don't leap into it. Nizan studied negative form. His hatred was a pearl diver. Nizan took the pearls and threw them to us, rejoicing that it was his lot to serve the common ends by so personal a work. Without changing its immediate objective, his private struggle against the particular dangers that threaten

---

* A quotation from a sonnet by Stéphane Mallarmé, *Ses purs ongles très haut dédiant leur onyx.* . . . (Trans.)

a young bourgeois became his public function. He talked about hate and impotent fury, he wrote about the Revolution.

Thus it was the Party that made the writer. But the man? Did he have his "field" at last? His fulfillment? Was he happy? I do not think so. The same things that deprive us of happiness render us forever incapable of enjoying it. And then, the doctrine was clear and confirmed his personal experience. His alienations were bound up with the present structures of society and would disappear with the bourgeois class. But he did not believe that he would live to see socialism or, even if he did catch a glimpse of it during the last days of his life, that there would be time for the world metamorphosis to transform the old habits of a dying man. Nevertheless, he had changed. Never again did he experience the old sense of desolation, never again was he afraid he was wasting his life. He experienced tonic rages, and joys. He was very willing to be only the *negative man*, the writer who demoralizes, who exposes the hoax. Was that enough to satisfy the grave child he had never ceased to be? In a sense, yes. Before joining the Party, he clung to his refusals. Since he could not be real, he would be empty, he would derive his sole value from his dissatisfaction, from his frustrated desires. But a feeling of numbness began to come over him, and he was terrified that one day he might let go and sink into consent. As a Communist he consolidated his resistances. Up until then he had always been afraid of social man as of a devouring canker. The Party socialized him painlessly. Its collective being was none other than his individual person. He had only to *consecrate* the swirling eddies within him. He thought he was a monstrous freak. They hoisted him onto the stage and he displayed his deformities saying, "This is what the bourgeois have done to their own children." Before, he had turned his violence against himself; now he made it into bombs and hurled them against the palaces of industry. The masonry was not damaged, but Nizan was liberated. He gave free rein to his sacred rage, but was no more conscious of it than a strong singer is of the sound of his own voice. The rebellious young man became a holy terror.

He did not liberate himself so easily from death, or rather from the shadow it cast across his life. But when he became an adult, the adolescent who had been consumed by another man's anguish earned the right to die on his own. Marxism revealed to him his father's secret: Antoine Bloyé's solitude came from his betrayal. This worker-turned-bourgeois was always thinking about "the companions he had had in the workshops along the Loire and in the booking-rooms at the railroad depots, companions who were on the side of the servants, on the side of life without hope. He used to say—and it was a remark which he later tried to forget but which disappeared only to reappear in the days of his decline, on the eve of his own death—'So I am a traitor.' And he was." He had crossed the line and betrayed his class only to find himself a mere molecule in the molecular world of the petty bourgeois. He regretted his desertion a hundred times over, and especially one day during a strike, when he stood watching the demonstrators march. "These men of no importance were carrying far away from him the strength, the friendship, the hope from which he was cut off. That evening Antoine reflected that he was a man of solitude. A man without communion. The truth of life was on the side of those who had never 'succeeded.' Those men are not alone, he thought. They know where they are going."

The turncoat had disintegrated, and now he was swirling in the bourgeois cloud of dust. He came to know the alienation and unhappiness of the rich because he had become the accomplice of those who exploited the poor. That communion with the "men of no importance" would have been a weapon against death. With them, he would have known the fullness of misery and friendship. Without them, he remained exposed: he was already defunct, a single sweep of the scythe had severed his human ties and his life.

Was Monsieur Nizan really this sorrowful deserter? I do not know. In any case, that is the way his son saw him. Nizan discovered, or thought he discovered, the reason why he opposed his father in a thousand little ways: he loved the man in him

and hated the betrayal. I invite the well-meaning Marxists who
have studied my friend's case and explained it by an obsession
to betray, to reread his works with their eyes open, if they still
can, and not to hold out against the obvious truth. It is true
that this son of a traitor often speaks of betrayal. In *Aden* he
writes: "I might have been a traitor, I might have suffocated."
And in *Les Chiens de garde*: "If we betray the bourgeoisie for
mankind, let us not be ashamed to admit that we are traitors."
Antoine Bloyé is a traitor to mankind. Another traitor appears in
La Conspiration, the unfortunate Pluvinage, son of a cop and a
cop himself. And so what does it mean, this oft-repeated word?
That Nizan sold out to Daladier? When they start talking
about other people, the members of the Left Establishment in
France are shamefully ready to be shocked. I know of nothing
dirtier and more puerile, unless it is "decent" women gossiping
about a free woman. Nizan wanted to write and he wanted to
live. What need had he of thirty miserable pieces of silver drawn
on secret funds? But as the son of a worker who had become a
bourgeois, he wondered what he really was: a bourgeois or a
worker? There is no doubt that his chief preoccupation was this
civil war inside him. A traitor to the proletariat, Monsieur Nizan
had made his son into a traitor to the bourgeoisie: the bourgeois-
in-spite-of-himself would cross the line in the other direction.
But that is not so easy. When communist intellectuals feel like
joking, they call themselves proletarians: "We do manual labor
at home." Lacemakers, so to speak. Nizan was more lucid and
more demanding. He saw in them and in himself petty bourgeois
who had sided with the working class. There is a gaping gulf between a Marxist novelist and a skilled laborer. They smile
prettily at each other across it, but if the author takes a single
step he falls into the abyss. That's all very well for a bourgeois,
the son of a bourgeois and the grandson of a bourgeois—having
your heart in the right place can't change the facts of birth. But
Nizan was a blood relative of his new allies. He remembered his
grandfather who had remained "on the side of the servants, on
the side of life without hope." Nizan had grown up like the

children of railroad workers, in landscapes of iron and smoke. But an engineering diploma had sufficed to plunge his childhood into solitude, to impose on his entire family an irreversible metamorphosis. Never did he cross the line again. He betrayed the bourgeoisie without going over to the enemy camp, and like "The Pilgrim," he had to remain with one foot on either side of the border.* Till the very end he was the friend of "those who had never 'succeeded,'" but he never managed to become their brother. No one was to blame except the bourgeois who had made his father into a bourgeois. This discreet void always bothered him. He had heard the bourgeois sirens, and because he was conscientious he was always worried. Since he could not participate in the "communion of servants, of those who live without hope," he never thought he was sufficiently protected against temptation, against death. He shared in the camaraderie of the Party members but he never escaped from the solitude that was the heritage of a betrayal.

His life would not be stolen from him. Once he was delivered from another man's death he saw his own: it would not be the death of the general foreman of a railroad yard. But this negative man, deprived of the humblest fulfillment, realized that in the end he would suffer an irrevocable defeat. When he was gone, nothing would have happened except that a refusal would have disappeared. A very Hegelian demise, in sum—it would be the negation of a negation. I doubt that Nizan derived the slightest consolation from this philosophical view. He made a long trip to the USSR. Just before he left he told me what he hoped to find. Out there, perhaps, men were immortal. The abolition of classes filled in all gulfs. United by a long-range undertaking, workers transformed themselves through death into other workers, those workers into still others, and the generations would succeed each other, always different and always the same.

---

* An allusion to Charlie Chaplin's silent film *The Pilgrim* (1922). In the last scene, Chaplin, in order to escape both Mexican bandits on one side of the border and U.S. police on the other, walks away with one foot on either side of the line. (Trans.)

He came back. His friendship for me did not entirely preclude a little enthusiastic propagandizing. He told me that the reality surpassed all hopes. Except on one point: the Revolution delivered men from the fear of living, but not from the fear of dying. He had questioned the best people. They had all replied that they thought about death and that their zeal for the common task did not save them from that obscure personal disaster. Disillusioned, Nizan renounced forever the old Spinozan dream: he would never know the affirmative plenitude of the finite mode which at one stroke breaks through its boundaries and returns to the infinite substance. In the midst of the collective commitment, he would retain his individual anxiety. He tried not to think about himself any more, and succeeded in keeping his mind on objective necessities. But because of this hollow, indissoluble nothingness, this bubble of emptiness inside him, he remained the most fragile and "most irreplaceable" of men. A few scattered sentences show that, individualized in spite of himself, in the end he chose the most individual solution: "It takes many capabilities and many creations for a man to escape nothingness. . . . Antoine understood at last that he could have been saved only by what he might have created, by the exercise of his powers." Nizan was not an engineer. Nor a politician. He was a writer. The exercise of his powers could only be an exercise in style. He put his faith in his books, he would live on in them. At the heart of this disciplined existence, which daily grew more militant, death placed its cancer of anarchy. For better or for worse, that lasted ten years. He devoted himself to his Party, lived dissatisfied, wrote passionately. A gust of wind blew out of Moscow—the trials—shaking but not uprooting him. He stood firm. No matter: he was a revolutionary but he was not blind. It was his virtue and his weakness to ask for everything *right now*, as young men do. This man of negation never resigned by acquiescing. On the subject of the trials he held his peace, that was all.

I considered him the perfect Communist. It was convenient:

in my eyes he became the spokesman for the Party's Political Bureau. I took his moments of ill temper, his illusions, frivolities, and passions for attitudes agreed upon in high places. In July of '39, in Marseille, where I met him by chance and for the last time, he was gay. He was about to sail for Corsica. I read in his eyes the gayety of the Party. He talked about the war, thought that we would escape it. I instantly made a mental translation: "The Political Bureau is very optimistic, its spokesman declares that the negotiations with the USSR are going to be successful. By fall, he says, the Nazis will be on their knees."

September taught me not to confuse the opinions of my friend with the decisions of Stalin. I was surprised. Annoyed. I was apolitical and reluctant to make any commitment, but my heart was on the Left, of course, like everyone else's. Nizan's rapid rise had flattered me and given me a sort of revolutionary importance in my own eyes. Our friendship had been so precious, and we were still so often mistaken for each other that it was I as much as he who was writing the lead articles on foreign policy for *Ce Soir*, and that was one subject I could tell you a thing or two about. If Nizan really didn't know anything, what a comedown for us both—that would mean we were just a couple of poor clods like the rest of the rank and file. Unless he had deliberately deceived me. That conjecture amused me for a few days: I had believed him, I was an idiot. But he retained his important functions, his perfect knowledge of what we used to call "the diplomatic chessboard," and at heart I preferred it that way. A few days later I learned from the papers, in Alsace, that the spokesman for the Political Bureau had just quit the Party, giving considerable publicity to the rupture. So I had been wrong about everything from the beginning. I don't know what prevented me from falling into a stupor—my insignificance, perhaps. And the fact that at the same time I was discovering the monumental mistake of a whole generation—our generation—that had fallen asleep standing up. We were being pushed toward massacres, through a savage pre-war period, and we thought we were stroll-

ing on the lawns of Peace. In Brumath I lived out the days of
our immense, anonymous awakening. At last I lost my sense of
distinctiveness, and I lost it for good. I was absorbed.

Today I can look back on my apprenticeship without distress,
but I know that at that same time Nizan was *unlearning*. How
he must have suffered! It is not easy to leave a political party.
There is a law that you have to wrench out of yourself and smash,
there are men whose familiar, beloved countenances will become
the snarling faces of the enemy, there is the dark mass of humanity that will stubbornly continue to march, grow distant and
disappear. My friend was an interpreter, and found himself
alone, in the North, in the midst of English soldiers—alone
among the English, as he had been during the worst period of his
life, when he was in Arabia, fleeing under the sting of the gadfly,
separated from everyone and saying "no."

Of course he gave political explanations. His former friends
accused him of moralism. He reproached them with not being
Machiavellian enough. He said he approved of the sovereign
cynicism of the Soviet leaders; all means were legitimate to save
the fatherland of socialism. But the French Communists had
neither adopted the cavalier stance of the Soviets, nor understood that they must give the appearance of breaking with them.
They would lose their influence because they had not promptly
mounted a show of indignation.

Nizan was not the only one to use these arguments. How flimsy
they seem today! In reality, he fell back on Machiavelli only as
a retort. He wanted to prove he was a realist. As a tactician, he
was condemning a tactic. That was all. And most particularly, no
one was to think he was quitting the Party in a rage, or because
of some emotional disturbance. But his letters prove he was
overwhelmed with anger. Today we know more about the circumstances, we have the documents, and we understand the
motives behind Soviet policy. I tend to think that he acted
impulsively, that he should not have broken with his friends,
with his true life. I tell myself that if he had lived, the Resistance
would have brought him back into the ranks, as it did so many

others. But that is not what concerns me here. I want to show that he was mortally wounded, stricken to the heart; that this sudden shift revealed to him his own nakedness and sent him back to his desert, to himself.

He wrote the foreign policy pieces for *Ce Soir*. One theme only: unite with the USSR against Germany. He had developed it so often that he had become convinced of it. While Molotov and Ribbentrop were putting the finishing touches on their Pact, Nizan was shouting himself hoarse demanding, with threats, a rapprochement between France and the USSR. During the summer of '39, in Corsica, he saw some of the leaders. They were friendly to him and congratulated him on his articles. But at night, after he had retired, they held long secret confabulations. Did they know what was in store for us? Nothing is less certain. The Party, still in the middle of vacation, was thunderstruck by the revelation of September. In Paris frightened journalists blindly assumed the gravest responsibilities. In any case, Nizan never doubted for a moment that he had been lied to. It was not his vanity that suffered, or even his pride—he had been wounded much more deeply: in his humility. He had never crossed the frontier between the classes and he knew it. Not trusting himself, he saw the silence of the leaders as evidence that the people did not trust him. Ten years of obedience had not allayed their suspicions. They would never forgive this doubtful ally for his father's betrayal.

The father had worked for others, for gentlemen who robbed him of his strength and life. In reaction against that, Nizan had become a Communist. Now he was learning that they had used him like a tool, hiding the real objectives from him. They had fed him lies and he had repeated them in good faith. He too had been robbed of strength and life by distant, invisible men. It had taken all his stubbornness to refuse the sweet, corrosive words of the bourgeoisie, and now again, in the very Party of the Revolution, he suddenly came upon the thing he feared the most: alienation from language. The communist words that were so simple, almost crude—what were they after all? Hot air. He had written of his father that he had performed "solitary acts dictated by an inhuman, outside power . . . acts which had not been part of an authentic human existence, which had had no real consequences. They were acts which were merely recorded in dusty files done up in string . . ." Now he remembered the acts which *he* had performed as a Party member, and they were twin brothers to the acts of the bourgeois engineer—they had had no "real consequences." A few scattered articles in dusty newspapers, empty phrases dictated by an outside power, the alienation of a man from international politics, a life without weight or substance, a "hollow image of that headless creature who strode with hurried footsteps through the ashes of time, without direction, without landmarks."

He came back to his eternal preoccupation. He had joined the Party in order to save his life, and the Party robbed him of life; he was fighting for the Party in order to stave off death, and death came to him through the Party. I think he was mistaken. The massacre was brought forth from the womb of Earth and it sprang to life everywhere. But I am talking about what he thought: Hitler, his hands freed, was going to throw himself upon us. Nizan imagined that our army of workers and peasants was going to be exterminated with the consent of the USSR, and he was stupefied at the thought. To his wife he spoke of another fear: the war would be interminable, and when he came back it would be too late, he would be worn out. He would survive only to brood over his regrets and his bitterness, haunted by the counterfeit coin of memories. In the face of these re-awakened threats, the only thing left was revolt, the old, anarchic, desperate revolt. Since everything betrayed mankind, he would preserve what little humanity was left by saying "no" to everything.

The angry soldier of 1940 with his set opinions, his principles, his experience, with all his instruments of thought, bears little resemblance to the young adventurer who set out for Aden. He wanted to reason, to see clear, to weigh everything, to preserve his ties with "those who had never 'succeeded.' " The bourgeoisie was waiting for him, affable and corrupting. He had to outwit it. Betrayed, as he thought, by the Party, once again he felt it his duty not to betray in turn. He insisted on still calling himself a communist. He reflected, patiently: how does one correct deviations without lapsing into idealism? He kept notebooks and records, he wrote a great deal. But did he really think that all by himself he could correct the inexorable movement of those millions of men? A lone communist is lost. The truth of his last months was hate. "I want," he wrote, "to fight real men." He was thinking of the bourgeois, but the bourgeois have no faces. The face you think you hate fades out and in its place you find Standard Oil or the Stock Exchange. Till the day he died, Nizan nursed grudges against particular persons: this friend had been too much of a coward to support him, that one had encouraged him to make the break and then condemned him for it afterward. He had vivid memories to feed his anger. He remembered eyes, mouths, smiles, the color of someone's skin, a severe or sanctimonious look, and he hated these faces that were all too human and familiar. If ever he experienced fulfillment, it was during those violent hours when he chose his victims and rage became a delight. When he was utterly alone, "without direction, without landmarks," and reduced to the inflexibility of his refusals, death came and took him. *His* death: idiotic and savage, the very death of which he had always had a dread foreboding. An English soldier took the time to bury his private notebooks and his last novel, *La Soirée à Somosierra*, which he had almost completed. The earth swallowed this testament. When in 1945, on the basis of exact information as to their whereabouts, his wife tried to recover his papers—the last lines that he had written about the Party, about the war, or about himself—nothing was left of them. About that time the slander campaign began in earnest, and the dead man was condemned for high treason. What a strange life: alienated, then stolen, then hidden, and saved even in death because it said "no." An exemplary life too, because it was an outrage, like all the lives that young men have been made to live, like all the lives that are being manufactured for them today. But it was a conscious outrage that publicly denounced itself as such.

Here is his first book. They thought he had been obliterated; he comes to life again because a new public demands him. I hope that we shall soon see his two masterpieces in print again: *Antoine Bloyé*, the most beautiful, the most lyrical of funeral orations, and *La Conspiration*. But it is not a bad thing to begin with this naked revolt. At the beginning of everything there is first of all refusal. Now let the old men depart and leave this adolescent to speak to his brothers: "I was twenty. I will let no one say it is the best time of life."

JEAN-PAUL SARTRE

March, 1960

Aden, Arabie

by Paul Nizan

In general, one must not consider a journey to Arabia as a pleasure trip. But he who wishes to become acquainted with foreign lands and who hopes thereby to improve his fortune once he has returned home, must resign himself to some unpleasantness.

Young men who like their comforts and a dainty table, or who wish to pass their time pleasantly in the company of women, must not go to Arabia.

—Carsten Niebuhr, *Description of Arabia* (1774)

I

I was twenty. I will let no one say it is the best time of life.

Everything threatens a young man with ruin: love, ideas, the loss of his family, his entrance into the world of adults. It is hard to learn one's part in the world.

What was our world like? It was like the chaos the Greeks put at the beginning of the universe in the mists of creation. Except that we thought it was the beginning of the end, the real end, and not the one that is the beginning of a beginning. Faced with exhausting transformations which only an infinitesimal number of witnesses were trying to understand, all one could perceive was that confusion was leading to the natural death of what existed. Everything resembled the terminal disorder of a disease: before death, which renders all bodies invisible, the unity of the flesh is dissipated, each of the parts pulls in its own direction. It ends in a decay that knows no resurrection.

Very few men felt they saw clearly enough to sort out the forces that were already at work behind the great, decaying debris.

We knew none of the things we would have had to know. Culture was too complicated for us to understand anything but the ripples on the surface. The professional intellectuals were wearing themselves out with subtleties in a world of reasoned arguments, and almost none of them was capable of so much as spelling out the words in the texts they discoursed upon. Error is never so simple as the truth.

They needed to know the ABC's of what was really important. But instead of learning to read, the ones who lay awake at night, tormented by real anxiety, imagined various conclusions, all based on studies of decadent societies of the past: the invasion of the barbarians, the triumph of machines, apocalyptic visions, recourse to Geneva and to God. How intelligent everybody was!

But these clever men were too near-sighted to look up over their glasses and see beyond the shipwrecks. And the young people trusted them.

Absolute condemnations, sentences that could not be appealed: "You are going to die." The young people of my age, prevented from catching their breath, suffocating as though their heads were being held under water, wondered if there was any air left anywhere. Nevertheless they had to be sent to join their drowned families beneath the surface.

Since I was classed as an intellectual, the only people I had ever met were technicians without inner resources: engineers, lawyers, archivists, professors. I can no longer even remember such utter poverty.

Prudent advice, and the chances of my academic career, had brought me to the École Normale and that official exercise which is still called philosophy. Both soon inspired in me all the disgust of which I was capable. If anyone wants to know why I remained there, it was out of laziness, uncertainty, and ignorance of any trade, and because the state fed me, housed me, lent me free books, and gave me an allowance of a hundred francs a month.

The École Normale is the envy of other nations. It is one of the heads of France, which has as many heads as a hydra. It trains part of the proud troupe of magicians whom those who pay for their schooling call the Élite, and whose mission it is to keep the people in the path of complaisance and respect, which virtues constitute the Good. At the École Normale there reigns the *esprit de corps* of seminaries and regiments: it is easy to make young men believe that their individual self-effacement contributes to collective pride, that the École Normale is a real being with a soul—a beautiful soul—that it is a moral person more lovable than truth, justice, and men. In this place, inhabited, like the Garden of the Rose, by transparent creatures, Hypocrisy is queen.* Most of the students think of themselves only in terms

---

* An allusion to the *Roman de la Rose*, a long allegorical poem dating from the thirteenth century, in which the Rose growing in the garden of the god of Love symbolizes a lady, and the progress of her Lover's suit is variously helped or hindered by such characters as Pity, Generosity, Fear, Jealousy, etc. (Trans.)

that affirm their membership in the élite. The Christian élite: many of them love the mass. The academic élite: some of them prepare the successive stages of a fine career as if it were a great journey, and at the age of twenty make plans to marry the daughters of famous professors—the *Bulletin de l'École Normale* publishes proud and laughable genealogies. The political élite: several of them swim in the muddy waters of the Socialist clubs and the Radical leagues as skillfully as old fish. And always, the intellectual élite. Most of their meditations on the value of men never go beyond the limit of these ambitious thoughts.

To adolescents worn out by years of lycée, corrupted by the humanities and by the bourgeois morality and bourgeois cooking of their families, the École offers the example of illustrious predecessors: Pasteur, Taine, Lemaître, Giraudoux, François-Poncet. It promises students that they too will receive the Legion of Honor and be elected to the Academy at the end of their days. But no one tells them about the life of Évariste Galois.*

In 1924 there was still one man at the École: Lucien Herr. When you saw that giant bent over a mountain of books, his clear eyes peering from beneath a bulging forehead, from beneath a steep cliff of thoughts, when you heard his voice that never lied pronounce judgments with the sole object of rendering to each his due, you knew that you were safe in that filthy abode. But he died. The École Normale remained, a ridiculous and, more often, odious thing, presided over by a patriotic, hypocritical, powerful little old man who respected the military.

For years, on the Rue d'Ulm and in the lecture halls of the Sorbonne, I listened to important men who spoke in the name of the Mind.

---

* A brilliant young mathematician (1811–1832) who made important contributions to the theory of algebra. His genius was unrecognized during his lifetime and his work was repeatedly ignored or rejected by the Academy of Sciences. An ardent Republican and outspoken enemy of Louis-Philippe, he was expelled from the École Normale for political activity and thereafter lived in abject poverty. He was arrested and imprisoned as a dangerous agitator and, at the age of twenty-one, was killed in a pistol duel under circumstances suggesting that his adversary was an *agent provocateur* of the police. (Trans.)

They were the sort of philosophers who teach wisdom in scholarly journals and write books full of footnotes and sound arguments. They join learned societies and convene congresses to determine what progress the Mind has made in the course of a year, and what remains to be accomplished. They wear ribbons on their lapels like old, retired gendarmes. They dedicate marble plaques at crossroads in Holland, or on houses where somebody was born or where somebody died. These commemoration ceremonies give them the opportunity to travel. Nearly all of them live on the west side of Paris, in Passy, or Auteuil, or Boulogne, quiet districts where there are few noises and few men, and where girls do not become pregnant before they are married. They are the Wise Men of the 16th arrondissement.

They present orderly ideas, finely honed theories on psychology, morality, and progress—abstractions which were already threadbare in the days of Jules Simon and Victor Cousin but which apparently still have a lot of wear left in them. These philosophers are simple fellows who say that truth must be caught on the wing like an unsuspecting bird. They issue pronouncements on war and peace, on the future of democracy, on justice and God's creation, on relativity, serenity, and the spiritual life. They make up vocabularies, because they have all discovered one important proposition: when the terms of problems have been adequately defined, problems will no longer exist. They will fall to dust. To state a problem will be to solve it without further examination. Philosophers will simply be watchdogs of vocabulary, and historians of the Dark Ages when words had several meanings. In the meantime, they learn to set aside dangerous thoughts until the day when the poison in those thoughts has evaporated. Reason can afford to wait, she will come back to them in her own good time, which does not coincide with the time of men.

Thus they practice philosophy—which, after all, demands enough orderliness and care so that it is an honorable calling for men who might have been accountants or Jesuits.

And what language! They display so many finely turned

phrases, so many proverbs and figures of speech, that I am not sure I will ever be able—even with the help of silences filled with the secret teachings of sleep, and of conversations with passers-by in the public squares, or in barracks, bistros, and factories—to rediscover the meaning of the straightforward words and simple expressions invented by men.

One great thinker among them: Léon Brunschvicg. Playing his cards closer to the chest, and hiding more aces up his sleeve. Because he had the precision of a watchmaker and the adroitness of a conjurer, you thought at first he was a philosopher. But in the end you found only a Robert Houdin* whose measure you could take, whose lies you could count. This little retailer of sophisms had the physical appearance of an old maître d'hôtel who late in life had been permitted to grow stout and wear a beard. Guile lurked in the corners of his eyes and guided the short, insipid movements of his hands, the hands of a Jewish merchant. Winking, letting fly his witticisms as though they were decrees of reason, suggesting in every speech: leave it to me, everything is going to be all right, I can fix everything, both in souls and in the sciences. Then bowing to the audience. What a hidden appetite for position, for rest and honors! What a real terror of the truth which poses a threat, the truth which, for example, might have placed in jeopardy this rich man's money! The disciples ranged around him held themselves in readiness to raise above his corpse the mercenary banner of critical idealism.

But men were working on the assembly line, policemen were walking the streets. In China men were dying violent deaths, in Upper Volta forced labor was felling the Negroes like an epidemic.

They did what they could to hide from us the flesh-and-blood existence of our brothers, in order that we might be well armed for the tasks we were destined to perform—the tasks of curés. The bourgeoisie coops up its intellectuals and force-feeds them

---

* A French magician (after whom the famous Houdini named himself) celebrated in the nineteenth century for his optical illusions and mechanical devices. (Trans.)

like poultry in order that they may not be tempted to love the world. We lived at the dull speed of sleep: everyone knows it is the high speeds that are dangerous. We moved about as we had been taught to do, busying ourselves with the little construction games these functionaries taught us. There were people all around us, in the suburbs and the countryside. But we kept our eyes on our teachers, to do as they did, and also on our fathers, sadly crouched in corners, getting up occasionally to make their bosses laugh or to deliver to them a consignment of illusions, arguments, or justifications. Clowns and accomplices: the intellectual professions. From time to time they begged us to be patient: the world was about to be saved.

II

Imagine it: There we were at the age of twenty, let loose in a pitiless world, armed with a few graceful accomplishments— Greek, logic, an extensive vocabulary that did not even give us the illusion of understanding. We were lost in a dimly lit museum of our fathers' works, where in every corner we saw the vague outline of a bloody encounter: wars in the colonies, White terror in the Balkans, assassinations in America applauded by everyone in France. The terrible hypocrisy of the men in power could not obscure the existence of calamities we did not understand; we knew only that the calamities were there, that they were occurring somewhere. Do not tell us it was for our own good. Do not be content to blame it on fate, to eternally perform the gesture of Pilate.

On awakening in the morning, each man finds himself confronted with the great disorders of the time, reduced in scale to the petty dimensions of a personal anxiety. We have within us divisions, alienations, wars, debates. We were told we were living in the age of the guilty conscience, but that did not keep us from fearing for our lives, from suffering from the mutilations that awaited us. After all, we knew how our parents lived—in awkward misery, like cats with a fever, like seasick goats. Where was our sickness? In what part of our lives? We knew one thing: men do not live as men should. But we still did not know the elements of which a real life is composed; all our thoughts were negative. The celebrated philosopher Alain did indeed tell us: "To think is to say no." But only the Spirit of Evil says no eternally. The time will come when the mind will no longer fear the things it believes in; then man will be ashamed to have remained on the defensive so long.

We were dissatisfied in advance with the professions for which we were being trained, professions that did not even promise decent wages. We were afraid of what was going to happen to us. A fine youth! How could we seek the help of men? Where were they hiding? Everything set them apart from us: duty, family, country, respect, money—there were too many enemies. I have learned since that those enemies are only phantoms, reflections ten thousand times distorted that we took seriously because we were full of good intentions. But it took me a while to figure that out.

This was the way we felt: we were about to enter a prison and we were unable to imagine in detail what it would be like. What young man thinking about prison can guess what goes on in each cell? At the age of twenty a man cannot lay his hand on particular things, on individual events. But we had enough forebodings about the future to suffocate. And the things we feared were not illusions: we were threatened with real diminutions, with real constraints we could not begin to enumerate. In vain did you try to make us believe in the simple conflicts between freedom and determinism, predestination and grace, maturity and puberty. If it had been merely a question of words, we were just as clever as you, we too could have written scholarly papers and preached from rostrums. There were agonizing realities behind all your maxims.

But we were weak, we were impotent. Beginning with our comfortable childhood, we had been raised for docile slavery. We had no way of locating the hidden springs of hope within us. We had no divining rods, no way of knowing that we were suffering because our human capacities were idle. Our masters seemed unshakable, the machines that flattened every existence seemed too solidly constructed for us to break. But if we did nothing, the idleness would last all our lives. What was going to happen to us? What was *not* happening to us already? It is hard to be a compass crazed by a storm or an aurora borealis, spinning toward the cardinal points, in a darkness split by bells, flashes of light, and cries, where at every street corner madness struts and shows her comely face.

Our childhood had a lot to do with it. The eider-down quilts of provincial life, our first communion, the wisteria of the summer of '14 did not prepare us for war. The death of our cousins and brothers, the license afforded by the absence of our fathers, the murderous objects in the hands of older men, all these mysterious things provided food for our disorder. It was the disorder of a childhood miraculously unhampered by the restrictions of order: the war enabled us to live. There was no constraint other than the obligation to remove one's hat before the flag or in the presence of the dead. During air raids, when the night blazed with bombs, sirens, and conflagrations, and dogs howled in cellars, the children played and left their parents in peace.

Relying on the disasters of the time to mold heroic hearts and the love of virtue, our mothers and teachers took no great pains to instill in us the moral values that rose like a flood during the war. They thought we would acquire them as a matter of course, that we would breathe them in with the public-spirited air of wartime that circulated in even the remotest prefectures of the South. Thanks to so gross an error, we arrived at manhood ignorant of life. But it was too late to start drumming Laws into our heads like advertisements against syphilis. How could we believe in them? To us they were only fearful chains for a man, chains that cut into our lives. To be a man seemed to us to be the only legitimate enterprise. We were in despair when we discovered that all those noble duties, which they should have made us believe in ten years earlier, crushed out the love of life. Love the life they made for us? Put together provincial families, school examinations, well-bred young ladies, the low faces of drill sergeants, whores leaning on imitation marble, black avenues, lessons at thirty francs an hour, and Kant's table of judgments, and you are a man. What more do you need to fill your young life to overflowing?

This life we had been tricked into living unfolded amid the false atmosphere of national carnival that came into being immediately after the war. It was a life that began the morning of the armistice, the only time I ever saw people celebrating in the streets. A great exhalation of breath that we had been holding for years in the depths of our lungs, desire for sex and drink, the natural right to light as many lamps as we pleased, to insult old enemies, the day when, for the first time in my life, in front of a wholesale butcher's on the Boulevard Montmartre, I kissed a girl on the mouth. The men who had fought were drained of all the war they had in them, but they maintained their flame as faithfully as the imbecilic gas under the Arch of Triumph. Bursting with the insolent pride of having been forced to make sacrifices, they exploited the country's dead before our eyes. The glorious corpses were put to good use, no part of them was wasted by the sinister pork-butchers who retailed the pieces to the public. They lived according to the military order they dreamed of perpetuating in a nation in turmoil, surrounded by enemies they invented for it every day. They impregnated every heart with a foul smell of combat, bivouac, and furlough. Behind this display of patriotic ideals, by which a few adolescents of good family were taken in, French industry was being organized, and preparations were being made for a civil war against the workers, who do not eat dead men. We still had no clear understanding of these stern truths, but we did sense that these people were only noisy defenders of the law, self-appointed prophets pointing out to us the path of duty. Their fables had nothing to do with us. We were looking for something to get our teeth into and they wanted to snatch the bread from our mouths. Hunger and weakness corrupted our words and our first actions; the books they gave us read as if they had been written in a cemetery. The political parties propositioned us in broad daylight. Our appeals went unheeded. We had to do something. But what?

What idle slaves do. We amused ourselves. We went drinking in bands: consoling nights. We went to the movies: there at least you have animal warmth, and you can pick up women, you can touch their knees in the dark. Into these tanks filled with sound and flashes of white lightning, men go to forget themselves. They come out stupefied by dreams and go off to lose themselves in the cubicles where they experience what Monsieur Bergson still dares to call life, with the eternal dripping of a faucet in the corner. We did as men do.

We knew other women, too. I used to go to see one who kept a dismal little bar on the Rue Saint-Jacques. Her husband, dried out by the winds of Argentina, traveled between Paris and London, absorbed in business transactions of a sort that are not defined in the commercial statutes. Between journeys he planted tricolored darts in a straw target. This young woman, refined out of the alluvial sludge of her native town, was only a bored body on the frontier of a desert, but with her knees spread, the black and white scissors of her thighs were enough to give temporary satisfaction to my love of freedom, during those years when a moist mouth was all it took to break the routine. I lost myself with her in a country without contours, closed in by the great, vertical panels of the night.

All this continued for months and months. They tried to make us believe it was only a part of growing up, but we knew there was no reason for this sort of life to come to an end, because all men lived as we did, turning this way and that like bats. Since we did not know about our companions in revolt, buried in the countryside and in the furnished rooms of Billancourt, our only thought was to run away. *They* stayed where they were, condemned to a slavery that was harder because it was also the slavery of the body: aching backs, and not enough meat and air. But we, from the depths of our bourgeois lives, how were we to guess that the foundations of our fear and slavery lay in the factories, the banks, the barracks, the police stations, in all the places that were unknown territory to us?

Each of us tried to escape in his own way.

III

There were many ways of escape—many doors leading no-where.

Some young men turned to God and his priests, asking them to explain what was wrong. They started out teaching the Lord's Prayer to children in the parochial schools and were soon carried away with it, mistaking humiliation for prayer and the ruination of man for saintliness. This made it possible for the more intelligent among them to devote themselves to a kind of poetry: God went about his business in his ancient way, letting himself be adapted to any recipe. Benevolent deities sprang up, saints appeared to poets who wanted people to think they were artists dedicated to the service of Our Lady. Sanctuary, indulgences, immense purity. Poets opened offices of conversion. Rimbaud, despite the efforts of his last defenders, was taken over by the church; curés, in order to gain acceptance by the young, explained that prayer and poetry are only different faces of the same act. This two-faced Janus opened the door to all possible statements about the purity and impurity of poetry, about inspiration, conversion, and reversion.

Others, inflamed by the lights of Paris, got used to dying in hovels, beset by the female images that haunted so many young men after the years of war. Men with nothing to do, they lived in a horrible state of false naiveté that was also called poetry, sunk in an evil whose causes they made no effort to confront. The phoenix named romanticism was thus reborn: literature was raised to the level of a tame god who was always available for communion. A *mal du siècle* as comfortable as spiritualism, a last refuge in which to die in peace amid the musty smell of châteaux abandoned by their grandfathers. But could their seriousness—the seriousness of sick adolescents—bring down the walls they could not climb, walls pierced by loopholes through which so many eyes were watching them? After all, there were other clowns in the service of the bourgeoisie who were already middle-aged and tormented each day by new signs of their decline. All this poetic reality helped the French industrialists, the academicians, the police, the clergy, the French socialists, to prevent their beloved class from dying. Let us hope, for the ultimate honor of man, that the poets suspected nothing.

Other doors led to great men. You immersed yourself in their lives, you participated in their glory as though you were at a movie or a Lenten service at Notre Dame. They were in fashion; you became one with them as you fell asleep, you knelt down in their calm, expiatory chapels, where one stopped thinking about prices on the stock exchange, about strikes, assassinations, and armies, about suitable marriages and conjugal duties. Saint Thomas picked up thin-blooded disciples in genteel families around Sainte-Croix de Neuilly and the Catholic Institute. So did Kant, Pascal, Descartes, and Louis XIV.

Then there was irony. Irony was proper and respectable, like a notary. At least it was patriotic, since it conformed to the national tradition: reticence is the virtue of these little Frenchmen. Irony frightens no one. It is not so negative as it seems, it will not prevent you from making a career for yourself that will be applauded in the best society. You can climb to the top wearing the label of "skeptic" that has been so honorable since Montaigne and Huet.

There remained real escape. That did happen: every so often we would read in the newspapers about a suicide. Then, with an American correctness, young men would organize an inquiry: Suicide—is it a Solution?

There were some who, having knocked at all these doors, found that the frozen reasons that still held them fast were beginning to melt. Recalling childhood games and things they had read, they suddenly remembered that people travel. During those soft years, in which disgust, and impatience to be men, rose in everyone like an attack of fever, an irresistible centrifugal force pulled the least weighty of them away from the center of the earth called Paris. They went spinning in all directions, toward whatever point of the compass seemed to offer a last chance. The promise of adventure reinforced the confidence in life that, despite everything, they could not help retaining. Adventure became the wondering attention they fixed on the future. These voyages rarely had a commercial purpose, and there was a good deal of naiveté in them. But there were excuses for the naiveté: writers and philosophers promised wonders from travel, it was a word overlaid with literary and moral adornments. The stain of morality spoiled everything.

No travel in Europe: we had come to regard the whole of that slim band of territories, that branch of Asia, as our native land. We spoke of it as a single entity, doomed to the misfortunes of a single destiny: there was our country—Europe—and us. It was the dust of Europe we had to shake from our feet. And elsewhere lay the other continents, overflowing with all the strength, virtue, and wisdom that our province lacked. Anything, we felt, was better than Europe, better than any part of it. And we were right, because the German cartels, the Fascist militia, the English textile mills, the Rumanian executioners, and the Polish socialists cast a shadow as black and cold as the shadow of the French steel trust and the factories of Saint-Gobain. But we knew nothing about all that. We were thinking in terms of the inner life when we should have been thinking in terms of dividends. You must understand that we were in the grip of indefinable yearnings, that we were swept up in a whirlwind of sentimental appearances. We had been educated badly enough, artificially enough, so that we could think about Justice, Good, and Evil with a straight face. After all, we were living in a dream, but all the forces in us were pulling us back to earth.

So we would cross the borders of this peninsula bounded by water and the frontier stakes of Russia. We would condemn this molehill with its heaps of slag, the refuse of its ancient mines. The professors themselves, patient accomplices of the poets, were discussing its decline, philosophers were describing the decadence of the West. How were we to know that the real decadence of the world was manifest everywhere, in colonial wars, in American factories, in African trading posts. How were we to know that one day everything could begin anew, that everything was already beginning anew in the Soviet assemblies, in the workers' movements, in the upheavals that were bringing paralytic old Asia to her feet.

Our conclusion was worthless, because we had been taught to think of the East as the opposite of the West. So once it was established that the collapse and decay of Europe was a simple, inescapable fact, the renaissance and flowering of the Orient became a fact equally obvious. For Europeans, the Orient held salvation and a new life. It had medicine for our ills, and love to spare. We made free use of false analogies with antiquity and drew on the official history of religions. We endowed Asia with all the human virtues that had been gradually disappearing from the West over the last three hundred years, virtues that were no longer demanded anywhere outside the agony columns of the English dailies. The spirit of civilization hovered over India, China seemed more marvelous to us than it had to Marco Polo. Who was there to give us good, hard reasons for being interested in Asia: the strikes in Bombay, the revolutions and massacres in China, the jailings in Tonkin? Good, human reasons, instead of a reason like Buddhism.

There was also America.

Europe, with its meager portion of land, poor in men and oil, lacking in events, seemed to be an old and dying woman between two heroes: Asia, the hero of wisdom, and America, the hero of power.

Africa and the South Pacific were still only overflowing reservoirs of poetry, hardly utilized by anyone except traders in curiosities and poets whose inspiration had dried up.

All that only went to show how lazy the people of Europe were, and how powerless to do anything for themselves. Other continents supplied a few of the imaginary worlds into which they withdrew at night to forget the truth about their purgatory and to clothe their indigence and abasement with illusions.

IV

What else did the word travel contain? What was inside this Pandora's box?

Freedom, detachment, adventure, plenitude, everything that so many unhappy people lacked, everything that they possessed only in dreams, like Catholic adolescents dreaming of women. It contained peace, joy, the approval of the world and of oneself.

We modelled our lives after examples that had become venerable: Stevenson, Gauguin, Rimbaud, Rupert Brooke. Many writers were employed in the diplomatic corps, and the number and speed of international trains and the development of steamship lines placed travel within the reach of all.

The Parisians, who are sedentary as mussels, were moved by the posters of the P.L.M.* and the whistle of a train under the Pont de l'Europe just as the courtiers of Louis XVI were moved by the paintings of Watteau and the bleating of sheep. They yearned for travel in the same way that people of the eighteenth century longed for the country, for the blessed archipelagos, and journeyed to Ermenonville to read the pastoral works of Rousseau.

We have an almost unbroken tradition of travel, fostered by seafaring expeditions and popularized under the Republic by the development of free and compulsory education. Every schoolmaster encourages the love of foreign countries. This tradition is as commonplace as universal suffrage. It goes back as far as the early Renaissance, to a time when people were beginning to grow restive, when they were fascinated by stories of earthly paradises lost and regained, and by moral anecdotes about noble savages. They believed Christine de Pisan when, from the depths of her Middle Ages, she told them:

> *I went to the land of Brachyne,*
> *Where men are by nature good*
> *And do naught that is sinful or ugly.*

---

* A railroad line, the Paris-Lyon-Méditerranée. (Trans.)

Even before he reached his false America, Christopher Columbus saw rising from the Atlantic visions of the world of wonders. He landed on the islands: here—until the slaughter began—was the true home of human life that everywhere else was corrupt. For centuries people described imaginary voyages, as Plato had described the Isles of the Blessed. They thought they had reason to believe that somewhere in the world there was an Earthly Paradise. It was a country that had a longitude and latitude, the way to it had been forgotten, but with luck, its coordinates could be rediscovered through exploration. Beatitude and joy depended on geography. This belief persisted during the eighteenth century: pending the Revolution, utopias lay at the end of voyages. That is the point we are still at. Fourteen-year-old boys, suffocated by family virtue, fed up with crocheted antimacassars and woven grass rugs, break open the locked drawers of their parents. Respectable tradesmen, mechanized by existence, find their digestion troubled by the thought of the Lee-ward Islands and the Paradise Islands, the *Astrolabe* and the *Zélée*.* Some are naive enough to go—they actually leave for the South Sea Islands or the heart of Africa. And the intellectuals are no more sophisticated than the adolescents and the jewelers.

Except that as soon as the land has been explored, surveyed, and registered, the Europeans begin to exploit it. Everywhere one is robbed, as in a wood. The paradises turn out to be commercial enterprises in cobalt, peanuts, rubber, and copra; the noble savages are clients and slaves. The priests of all the white gods have set about converting these idol-worshipers, these fetishists. They talk to them about Luther and the Virgin of Lourdes and reveal to them the wonders of underwear from Esders' department store. With the Eucharist comes forced labor for the Compagnie Brazzaville-Océan. Thus are reduced

---

* Two ships commanded by the French navigator Dumont d'Urville (1790–1842), who twice circumnavigated the globe, exploring the coasts of Australia and the islands of the South Pacific and discovering the Adélie Coast of Antarctica. He was a national hero and his travel books were widely read. (Trans.)

to silence the very people from whom our fathers expected to learn secrets. All goes well: prayer and absinthe appear on the scene, and on the stock exchanges of the civilized world, colonial shares go up. The ones who, despite all the danger signs, land in Tahiti and the Marquesas find missionaries—so kind to the lepers—and tall, soft, syphilitic girls, Greek traders with bad teeth, and alcoholic NCOs who used to dream of spending their retirement as policemen in Saigon.

All that is left to be done is to conjugate the remaining utopias in the future tense, to bury them in the shining time to come, to invent, for the consolation of urban populations, the Never Land of the inner life.

But let me return to the world of the present and speak of real events.

There were, in this cruel time of which I speak, men who really wanted to escape from the dog kennels to which they were tied by chains of causes they hardly understood. They were not being hypocritical, they were not simply obeying literary slogans: they were not all intellectuals addicted to the delights of abstract reasoning. Nor idle amateurs who loved to sail on ruinous cruises. Nor anonymous businessmen. These flights were natural phenomena, like the crimes, marriages, and suicides of which there are such and such a number in a given country. The Powers that Be knew enough about these desires to use them for their own most brutal purposes: the recruitment of professional soldiers and sailors, the blood-stained peace of their colonial experiments. Articles in the colonial newspaper *Le Temps*, and recruiting posters on the doors of police stations, barracks, and municipal buildings, used crude tricks to exploit any desire that peasants, workers, and clerks might have to change their skins. Along with the certainty of bed and board, they promised the pleasures of the tropics and the easy virtue of women of color. They stole men's hearts by childish devices inspired by an elementary but working knowledge of human temptations.

Like everyone else, these travelers had been driven for years by methodical powers without understanding the first thing about their passions, movements, or words, about work or love. Years when everything was a military command, a regulation on the subject of discipline. Like everyone else, they had been victims of devils who made no allowance for the simplest human impulse to wander. Voices disquieting as the winds of March would come to them in the midst of their work, ordering them to go and meet events, to defy events to always pass them by. Events are not delivered to one's home, events are not a public utility like gas and water. But there are roads, ports, railway stations, there are other countries besides the familiar kennel: all one has to do is not get off at his subway stop one day. They realized that, with more or less clear understanding. They all belonged to that pitiful band of men who become aware of what starved lives they lead when, at the end of the day, they start home from their eternal work. How are they to use the unaccustomed idleness of their hands and the provisional liberty of the prisoners' exercise period? What games can they play? Where are the women, the friends who cannot be found, those things as simple as bread and water?

So they set off in search of unforeseeable events that would be more wonderful than comets in the year 1000, events that would make men of them. The only thing they were certain of was that their lives were empty, and that they themselves were restless shadows suffering from terrible humiliations.

It was high time for them to leave. Soon their eyes would no longer be capable of seeing the world, soon it would be too late for them to lay their hands on animals of flesh and blood, on three-dimensional objects, too late for them to prove to themselves that life in general was not the eternal waking sleep they had always known. They were feeling their way toward a discovery, an invention of something tangible, something like the Holy Cross, which they did not even desire clearly, because they had always slept and waked in a darkness so black that they could not even say what it was they wanted, the way one says I want a knife, or a dog, or God.

I wait among them, we are emigrants. I do not judge, the

whole method of clear thinking is out the window, I am trembling with anxiety. The door opens. Around me people are talking about the departure and giving me advice, I draw breath in a state of giddiness that was supposed to be agreeable. They bid me farewell, I slip away like a dead man.

V

I find myself one morning in the reddish light of October on the deck of a new little freighter that is raising anchor in a dock on the Clyde, at Paisley. The sun over the hoarfrost looks like the Japanese flag. In the fields the haystacks are frozen, the blades of grass must be as brittle as cracked glass.

When we have sailed down the Irish Sea, past Lundy Island, Europe falls into our wake like a buoy. Between Swansea and Cape St. Vincent, the *Amin* cuts the waters of the Atlantic amid the gales and squalls of the season. Through the windows of the chart room we can see heavy seas crash over the steering wheel and the figure of the man on watch; they make the ship's bell ring. In the cold sea damp the gulls, shielded from the wind, hover over the bridge, suspended on invisible wires. At night in the cabin the trunks bump against the walls, in the galley the set of dishes hung from the ceiling loses a cup, a plate. The bunks crack.

Monotonously, one after another, the promontories of Spain and Morocco appear like warnings, the heights, the warlike beehives of Gibraltar, Ceuta, Cádiz, Algeciras, Mount Ida. We follow them with our eyes until they are only a flat line of smoke on the horizon: we comment on them at length over the varnished table of the ward room.

In the waters of Malta British cruisers are on the prowl. Shots from cannon firing in target practice open deep caverns in the great, architectural silence of the sky. Between Malta and Crete one morning, a file of submarines slips by on the surface, like a school of porpoises tired of turning cartwheels. The traveler is reminded of Europe by the most revolting symbols of its destiny.

Having left Port Saïd with its women for sale, its boys to buy, its Syrian Jews, its amber waters, and the yellow steamers of the Peninsular and the British India swarming with coolies loading coal, the boat loses sight of the glass dome of the Compagnie du Canal, makes its way slowly between the sand dunes as far as Suez, passes Sinai, and heads into the Red Sea.

The thermometer rises every day, the suns turn, the days and nights finally melt into a glaring, leaden light that blinds our eyes. Sometimes the *Amin* passes under red and yellow cliffs broken at long intervals by white landmarks—the tomb of a holy man, or a ruined house. You would think you were on Mars: these are the watery boundaries of the desert.

The flying fishes slip by under the bow like frogs. Sometimes when we come near land, strange birds fly about the masts.

The peninsulas spread out over the water like the hands of dead men, and in the distance we see their high backbones. The sea is humped like a turtle, its waves uncurl and breathe with a sound of escaping steam. The sea moves like a jellyfish, it swells up, stretches out, retracts, blows out a vitrified protoplasm. It is not like a capricious woman but like the most primitive of animals.

One morning we see palm trees, short-legged as basset hounds, and metal cranes and red roofs. This apparition is Port Sudan. Along the quays, schools of sharks turn over on their backs, clumsily, and beg for food like bears; at night, dazzled by our searchlights, they perform ballets like wasps. They are like all other animals.

British Customs officers stand guard in long corridors lined with drums of gasoline. At the far end you catch a glimpse of curtains of red and white straw, and a black sky inhabited by vultures, arc-lights, and nebulae of the torrid zone.

We try to land. Convicts with heavy balls at their ankles are paving streets and watering trees fifty centimeters high. Sudanese are selling ivory cigarette cases, women's necklaces, leather whips. When we have had a drink at the metal-topped café tables we go back to the ship in order not to see the local functionaries playing bridge on the verandas of their houses, with women beside them. Then there is the unbearable weight of bittersweet tunes that the wireless operator plays all evening long on the bagpipe. He is trying to summon up for his comrades Scottish ghosts to people the void of the tropical seas. I didn't come here for séances with a medium.

Crouched in the stern, East Indian crewmen talk rapidly in low voices late into the night.

The dummy's hand is spread on the table; the blades of the fan, whirling like the wings of a great June bug, scatter the cards like leaves. Hands moist with sweat pick them up from among the scraps of raffia, the oil spots, the urine from sheep that have been unloaded.

We set out again, in the middle of that vast waterway, the Red Sea, moving away from the sultry port where we had already been overcome by the tropical condition: an inexhaustible rage, and sometimes a kind of sexual derangement. Three, four ships a day suffice to people this deserted route.

On the morning of the thirty-fourth day, a violet pyramid lifts itself up on the back of the Indian Ocean. It gets bigger from one minute to the next, like the plants that the fakirs make grow simply by looking at them. A flutter of flags. The pilot and the doctor arrive, the engines slow down. We discover houses that gradually assume the proportions of burrows where men live, a city in the shadow of masses of split rock. The anchor falls, a cloud of sand spreads out in the sea: latitude 12° 45′ North, longitude 45° 4′ East—this is Aden.

I have arrived. It's not much to boast about.

VI

At the end of a month of sea, of gales and ports and secrets whispered in the wind, I am beginning to understand parts of this journey. What is it? It is a fusion of the fine gray rains of spring and all the myths and legends about voyages: myths about how broadening travel is and how much one can profit from it, how much one gains from taking stock (for it seems that a voyage is an inventory—Duhamel said that to me before I took the train, and I wondered whether I wouldn't do better to give my ticket away to some poor stranger), legends about salvation, legends about freedom, which is supposed to roam the seas, legends about gentlemen of fortune. Not to mention the Jolly Roger. I have to leave that out because I don't know anything about it. After all, I never killed anybody.

Now that I am alone behind my square columns and my window-blinds made of reeds, I can sit quietly in an armchair built by a convict and think about my departure. I was afraid. My departure was the child of fear. When, from this distant latitude under the Tropic of Cancer, I look back on the years when I was nineteen and twenty—years I lived through with as much pleasure as one lives through a siege of typhoid or the grippe—I see a shameful fear breeding all the falseness and errors that a heart can hide. I am no better than the next man: I fled. The first impulse of fear is to flee. Call it cowardice if you will, but insults will not prevent young men from taking lizards for dinosaurs. On the day when the ship's sirens send up over the echoing docks their plumes of steam and their cries as of women in childbirth, travelers think they are going to receive, in exchange for what they are leaving behind, an unimaginable freedom of those basic human impulses that have been naked ever since Adam.

But what gifts does the ocean bring you when the days have passed, when you have crossed so many time zones you get muddled trying to think what your friends in Paris are doing, whether they are sleeping or eating?

You can say you are beyond reach, materially invulnerable. This is not a complicated idea. It means something very simple, yet very important: the old armature of the mind has been lost and a new one must be found—the mind cannot live without a framework. But this second birth does not occur automatically.

The armature of the mind is composed of objects of wood, metal, protoplasm, glass and cloth, cubes, spheres, living creatures, boxes, motors, visible appearances, tangible forms, noisy tunes. All at once you stop encountering horses and newspapers every five minutes, automobiles, women's cheeks, individuals wearing the Croix de Guerre, Corinthian buildings, library shelves, subway tickets. You stop encountering your life.

You also had a body—for the time being you still do. But perhaps only for the time being: you must not let it get away from you.

What a limbo one is in at sea, what a state of oblivion. How regular one's breathing is, as during sleep. The atmosphere is like that of a séance, there are phantoms all around, the great white ghost of Arthur Gordon Pym beckons to you. When the scientists tell us that sirens are really Indian sea-cows, I will laugh in their faces, because it's true: you find them around the corner of every wave, in every hidden recess of foam. And Nausicaä too, and even the Lotus-Eaters, even Circe with her wondrous charms. You cannot hear the voices of those talking machines called the family, or meet the people with whom you had a commerce of anger, distrust, and hypocrisy. You are asleep: the ideas, the threadbare forebodings, the trickery attached to objects in France sink away, like the last islands of Wales, into a distance so vast you would never have the courage to traverse it twice.

Finally, there is no one to take you to task for omissions and absences: just try, while still in your arrondissements and subprefectures, to forget your civic and filial obligations, your fraternal duties.

Man's whole diet—everything that nourishes him in another way than proteins and carbohydrates—is renewed. Surroundings slip by; surfaces shift, wrinkle, and roll toward the zenith; a ball of whirling fumes, fusions, signals, and electric waves suddenly dilates—what is there for the terrible old habits to cling to? The heritage of the land, city images, continental ways, everything is abruptly lost.

Nothing is solid any more except the ship, which is less solid than you think, a fish that can easily be disoriented. On land, when you walk across the floor, everything is connected to firm objects, which are constant enough so that you are not sorry to have learned in school about solid geometry and physics. Your legs don't have to bother about questions of balance.

All of a sudden, your body has to begin studying its movements. It is one year old, it has to invent its position every time the wind changes. At the same time it is losing its skin under the blazing sun of the tropics. The body is tumbling about and peeling: how can the mind find time to think about evil?

You can think only about simple, basic events when your limbs and eyes never encounter more than a trifling number of regular forms—a bridge trembling from waves and vibrations, two masts, a lateen yard, a compass, a Diesel engine.

As for the famous secret hidden in ships, he who lives on them will not find it. A flight of iron steps, slippery with oil and sharp-edged as bones, descends into the great belly of the hold. During the first nights, you wonder where it really leads. Beneath the level of the sea, which has no more reality than the level of a man's chest, or a man's hip? To the ocean deeps? Could one keep going, down to the retreats of extraordinary fish with their abdomens puffed up and their eyes on the ends of antennae, down to the red and green pennants of the seaweed? It would be a nice change to wander through a sort of prairie for sea-horses, spider-crabs, anemones. But you end up in a cattle-shed of boiling iron shaken by the vibration of machinery and the pulse of steam. It is the world, with its sealed doors to the right and to the left, its floors, its ceilings; there are pillars of red metal, pipes, ribs as on the inside of a thorax, rivulets of water with rainbows of oil, lamps swinging back and forth like pendulums. Do you think you can climb up to Saturn by endlessly extending the staircase of the Eiffel Tower? Top and Bottom. This Side Up. The world is only a packing case. You have to think seriously that you cannot go up into the sky or down under the water without an airplane or a diving suit, and that these mechanical violations of natural law last only for a time. That, in sum, is one meaning of human life: men have to take into account the facts of density and gravitational pull. That does not prevent them from living; this necessity is really no more important, as far as their happiness is concerned, than the fact that they have four limbs and only one head. In the end they even derive pleasure from it, once they have understood that there may be natural limits to the expansion and enrichment of man.

The bottom of a ship is a little world in the midst of a great, closed world, and—like the walls of the world—the walls of the ship set a limit on fantasies. Above the hold, the body lives in indolence, consumed by an impatience that has no objective.

All this represents various forms of laziness and oblivion. The so-called freedom of the seas is only absence.

But oblivion is not another name for freedom. And freedom is all that counts: I must retrace my steps. Back in Europe, on the quays of Glasgow where men did not have enough to eat every day (it was the time of the coal strike), I was looking for miracles, for events, for something that would be a break with the past and the promise of a real reincarnation. I was under the impression that human life could be discovered through revelation: what mysticism. But the men of my age lived in the expectation of something—anything. We had been taught to believe in fairy tales and we were waiting for the famous lightning-bolts of adventure.

Events do not wait for you around the bend, every turn in the road is not a gold mine. There is no such thing as a highway empty and monotonous as the plains of Champagne, without a village, and then suddenly when you're not thinking about it, without any warning, behind an outcropping of rock, the thing you were waiting for, the thing without a name. Mr. Barnstaple was driving alone one Saturday afternoon on such a highway.*

The people who make discoveries, those of whom one says, on reviewing their lives, that they were not born for nothing, are prudent, sedentary men, men who can stay awake patiently and remain in one place for a long time, men who hunt warily. Truth is brought down when you have been lying in wait for it, it is not a card that you turn up one evening in a game of chance in which every hand may be a winning one. If you want to live, you must rediscover perseverance. You want to live, yet you speed through your night like fragments of stars. You must pay attention by day and by night. While you are sleeping, all men may die. While you are running, you yourself may die.

A traveler is condemned to see only the multicolored walls—the merely architectural curiosities—of the houses in which sedentary men grow old. I was that traveler. To go back and forth on little steamers with peeling paint, or on native *dhows*, from one bank to the other of that deep canal of hell, to carom off the ramparts of Africa and Arabia—these disordered movements soon cease to resemble the ways of freedom. You feel a kind of metal ball turning inside your life: it knocks against your organs, and the more you move the more it hurts.

Windows are closed to travelers because wherever they go they think it incumbent on them to urge everyone else to travel. Naturally, everyone knows that travelers are the enemies of people who are able to stay for a long time in one room, and so, to travelers, other men are hermetically sealed. They keep on moving, expecting to receive happiness from benevolent chance, as if that tangled mixture of causes were a god who distributed rewards. But a stubborn man who is attached to a particular place, to a particular kind of action, and a consistent

---

* An allusion to H. G. Wells' novel *Men Like Gods* (1923), in which the hero, on rounding a bend on an ordinary country road one day, suddenly finds he has crossed into a utopian world of the remote future. (Trans.)

method—and yet whose passions have not been destroyed by that attachment—such a man can sort out causes and act on them. In order to be able to *abide*, in order to be able to say "my home" without blushing, it is therefore necessary to love true power. Real travelers and real fugitives are pitiful examples of human impotence.

There is only scanty truth in proverbs, but when one tells children that larks don't drop into your mouth ready-roasted, one is passing on to them a useful maxim, the simple thought that events do not fall from the sky.

Travelers have nothing to keep them alive except the surface of their bodies, their skin with its sensitivity to heat and cold, their sight, their hearing, their sense of smell. They are never released from idleness, not even by love, for women are forbidden to them. Women do not roam the roads. No living creatures are more patient, more anchored to one spot, than women. In almost perfect stillness they pursue profound activities about which they know practically nothing. I know a woman who has children, and who is unaware of the fact that she has ovaries. Travelers sometimes sleep with women they find at hand, women who happen to be aroused and as open as the mares in heat which, it is said, used to be offered to insemination by the winds. But these women do not follow the travelers, they are too absorbed in their eternal work. The travelers neither possess them nor are possessed by them; they only have the temporary use of bodies that are hostile to such impatient lovers.

How much patience it would have taken to win and know that woman I saw sitting in the sun in the garden of Gezira, along the Nile.

Traveler, wait until you find yourself more empty and trembling every day, sick because all of your movement only stirs up the pain inside you—then try and reassure yourself by repeating that you are free, that at least that cannot be taken away from you. The freedom of the roads and of the sea is completely imaginary. At the beginning of a journey it resembles freedom because you are comparing it to the terrible slavery of the life that went before. But all it really means is that you have license to execute certain physical movements and are no longer constrained to make gestures demanded by others. You experience an ease you have never known. The routes of land and sea are not densely populated, and those who live on them are not the sort to insist on one movement and forbid another. You can really expose your limbs to the air and give them room to move. There is no gesture that gets in someone's way, or is improper, or obscene, no crowd that your elbow may jostle. There are none of those shameful movements that people make in a crowd, such as slyly pressing against the hips of a woman, or secretly checking one's image in every mirror along the street, or turning aside to spit quickly into a handkerchief. You can urinate freely in the sea: are you going to call that freedom?

Freedom is the real ability and the real will to want to be oneself. The power to build, to invent, to act, to satisfy all the human capacities the exercise of which gives joy.

Travelers, like other people, are pulled in all directions by capacities that have no object to satisfy them: by love without a lover, friendship without a friend, fleetness without a course to run, power that never moves, strength that is never applied. They have no object, no purpose, no opportunity. They are as free as the sages who paralyze their human capacities one by one and call that mutilation wisdom. It is high time to stop being Stoics: you will have no heaven in which to make up for lost time.

To flee, always flee, in order to forget that you are mutilated?

This is no literary invention of mine. I once knew a soldier in the colonial troops who was being sent to the special disciplinary unit on Cape St. Jacques, and who said to his judges, stiff with gold braid: "It is impossible for me *not* to give in to the crises that come over me, to these flights that are the only crime you have to reproach me with. I have to flee. That is the only explanation I can give for what you call my habitual misconduct."

So I am at sea. I think these things about the sea in order to do her justice, to be fair to her, both for and against.

There is this absence, there are these disappearances, these eclipses of human beings who are drawn to a ship like moths to a lamp and then disappear, melting into the trembling heat of coral quays.

There is a huge, other existence placed heavily against us, a faceless world that crushes out the beating of our hearts. The sea and the desert, one element as mobile as fire, the other apparently immobile; these elements, these beings without voice, without mouth, without eyes, disfigured by burns, do not conspire against man. They are neither his allies nor his adversaries; he barely comprehends them with the help of geometry and calculus, for science is merely what prevents us from feeling lost. And yet when we approach them, images, desires, and ideas drop away one after another like flies killed by the approach of winter.

Freedom? It was not this emptiness I was seeking, but true power.

And what about sailors, who travel the world the way carpenters cut boards? There are still sailors, at sea, who are sometimes human.

Captain Blair performs real acts. When necessary, he rises to a kind of professional sublimity without thinking about it, without telling himself that the moment has come to be sublime. I once knew a poet who had been an apprentice in the merchant marine; he saved his eternal soul every time he threw a bucket of water on the bridge at five o'clock in the morning. Blair does not know he is saving his soul, but Blair commands. He struggles against sudden shifts of the wind, against squalls and currents, he is wary of reefs. He goes regularly from incident to incident without any complaisance for himself or any lyrical idea of the ocean. He knows that there are times when it won't do to twiddle his thumbs, when he has to make decisions and give orders, because everything depends on the speed and sureness of a few movements. He is beautiful to watch: one imagines him shouting to the director and the owner of his company, like the Master of the Storm: "Silence, you! To your cabins!" When his boat is new, like the *Amin*, Blair has an object to study: he learns how the oil pumps work, how this particular carcass obeys the turns of the wheel, how it behaves in a rolling sea. He listens to the noises of the ship as to a heart, until he knows it like a woman, until he is as tired of it as of an old wife.

He is complete when he is doing a man's work and has enemies to deal with: the colors of the sea-bottom, the different hues of the various cross currents. Then each member of the crew is an extension of his own body. Look at the foreman of a boiler factory commanding his men in front of the heavy stamping press, or watch a surgeon operating. Without any analysis that separates them from their action. That's the way Blair is, alive throughout the whole duration of his act: but he knows only one act, and that is his misfortune. The rest of the time—because you don't have a storm every day, or a difficult port—he is bored stiff, he regards his freighter as a prison cell, and he gets no consolation out of calling the sea a bitch. Any sentimentality about the sea would make him shake with his Scotch laugh: the sea is an unstable object, difficult to deal with and hard to understand; she is a vicious horse. She can kill with a damp and rotten death the man who forgets her at the instant when he should have remembered her ways. Blair does not even go ashore to contemplate the landscape: he has put in at Massawa twenty-five or thirty times, and he is not even interested in knowing that it is the most beautiful bay in the world, with its amphitheatre of mountains and its flat, yellow waters carrying streams of yellow sand, tangles of grass as in the Amazon, and blossoms from the tree I call the *flamboyant*. But he knows that at Massawa the *sheb*, or coral reef, extends out into the middle of the Red Sea. His navigation charts tell him that this maze of underwater streets, passages, and paths changes from year to year. He sees the foam along the lines of breakers, but he does not admire the "fields" of zoöphytes twenty-five meters away from him, with their buddings and blossomings. He knows only that it is not easy to navigate here: his action is directed to the point where it is most effective.

All these sailors are bored to death: Blair, who thinks about his dead children and about the German submarines his patrol-boat pursued through the icy mists of the North Sea in the autumn of 1917; Beaton; Hiddleston, the engineer, who dreams of signing onto a liner the way a civil servant dreams of being promoted to the next grade. There is not so much difference as one might think between a sailor and a traveling salesman who covers a territory in France in a Renault *six-chevaux*.

I tell you that all men are bored.

VII

Aden, Mukalla, and Muscat are amongst the hells that are mentioned in sailors' sayings.

—Élisée Reclus
The Earth and Its Inhabitants, Vol. IX

But only experience could teach the man I was then that moving through immense, anonymous space is no remedy for disorders that do not have spatial dimensions. Space even adds disorders of its own.

The most discerning travelers realize the truth about travel at their first port of call. Having left for Singapore or the Marquesas, they discover it before they have passed the Bitter Lakes and the desolate public squares of Suez. Only obstinacy, or necessities that have nothing to do with their own wishes, can force them to continue an itinerary from which they expect nothing but trouble.

I was not so discerning, and forgetting even the vertigo from which I had wanted to escape, I lived in Aden, that "ancient and celebrated city."

In the geography he wrote in 1683, Samson tells wonderful tales: "Zibit, near the tip of the Red Sea, is a beautiful city, well built and rich, and the seat of great trade in drugs, spices, and perfumes. It was the capital of a realm that was seized some six score years ago by the Turk, who also took Aden at the same time, hanging the king of Aden from the mast of his ship and beheading the king of Zibit. Aden is the pleasantest and most beautiful city in all Arabia. It is enclosed by great walls on the side of the sea and by mountains on the side of the land. On top of these mountains several castles are clearly visible. It has at least six thousand houses. It lies beyond the Red Sea, at the edge of the great ocean."

How impatient I had been in Paris three or four months

before my departure, when I read stories about the city where I was going to live. From my room I could hear the children shouting at their game of tag on the Rue d'Ulm. The taxis shifted gears. The cocks on the Rue Rataud crowed for rain at two in the afternoon. An oriole sat for hours on the top of a spindle-tree, swinging back and forth like an imbecile. A black-bird whistled the first measure of the *Marseillaise*. I was wild to be gone, I would wait until nightfall to go running through the streets of the Montagne Sainte-Geneviève.

And this is the place that is so beautiful you want to die looking at it.

Aden is a great, lunar volcano, one wall of which blew up like a powder keg before there were any men to invent legends about the explosion. They made the legend up afterward: the re-awakening of Aden, which is the mouth of hell, will announce the end of the world.

The trunk of a pyramid, baked to a purplish cinder in a blue world and crowned by the ruins of Turkish forts; a stone surrounded by concentric waves, dropped by the bird, Roc, at the edge of the Indian Ocean; a setting for the adventures of Sindbad the Sailor, connected to the great Arabian peninsula by an umbilical cord of salt marshes and sands, under a fierce sun indifferent to the prayers of men.

It is surrounded by deserts of water covered with jellyfish, that cast up sticks, razor-shells, helmet-shells, and fish. Between Ras Marshag and Khormaksar stretch whole banks composed of shells and the skeletons of strange fish that look like the veins of dried leaves. "At the change of the monsoons," says Reclus, ". . . myriads of fishes of every species are cast up dead on the beach at Perim and Aden."

Deserts of stone mark the beginning of Yemen, at the foot of a mountain range which is almost always floating in clouds of laundry. This mountain mass hides the fields of Arabia Felix, the gardens and palaces of Sana, and the dense populations of more than one legendary city.

Fortified patrol roads dominate the passes in the rock between the native city and the British city. There are black tunnels smelling of ammonia from excrement, villages of tombs, villages of houses, metal oil tanks, barracks overlooking the sea, airplane hangars, clubs, missions, the dust of disintegrating Christianity, a Masonic lodge, everything necessary for happiness.

The rocky roads bear camels laden with casks of water, trucks for sewage disposal, American automobiles driven by turbaned Somalis, English and Indian soldiers, mixed peoples. Aden was ever a market and a fortress: *emporium, vetissumum oppidum Aden*, said Claude Morisot in 1663.

Aden hums like some great, shaggy animal that has rolled in the dust and is covered with flies and gadflies. In the narrow alleys of the Bazaar crowds of people are squeezed between the walls of the street stalls, the pieces of silk roll off the hand looms like beautiful colored serpents, the Hindu moneychangers sitting in their doorways dressed in shining frock coats pour back and forth between their hands piles of rupees, sovereigns, and those Maria-Theresa dollars with which, about 1839, the English bought the edge of the peninsula.

Crouched near the doors of smoky little cafés, blissful men smoke water pipes and blow up their coals. Sometimes their backs are covered with cups made of goat's horn, to suck up diseased blood. The cafés are enormously important. They are one of the places where one attains *kief*. One can read the accounts of travelers of other times—the cafés at least do not change. They are described by Niebuhr, who visited Arabia around the middle of the eighteenth century:

"One sees no furnishings other than straw mats spread on the ground or on stone benches. On the chimney hearth stand copper coffee pots, well tin-plated within and without, together with a large number of cups. No refreshments are served in these oriental cabarets except a pipe of Turkish or Persian tobacco, and coffee without milk or sugar. Thus there is no opportunity for one to spend money or become intoxicated, the Arabs being as sober in these taverns as they were in the old days when they drank only water. . . . They do not like to stroll about, and often they remain for hours on end in the same place where they first sat down, without saying a word to their neighbors. They gather by the hundreds in these cafés. I confess that I have not often visited these houses. The European merchants dwelling in oriental cities never go there at all. Other travelers have even less desire to spend entire evenings glued to the same spot, particularly when they have no hope of hearing anything amusing."

Many native workers have no home and sleep in the open or in these cafés.

The Somalis play endless, noisy domino matches there. The Negroes all resemble the people of Marseille or Toulon.

The children in the Moslem school shout their verses in classrooms that are open like the shops; it doesn't seem to bother them. Beggars circulate. Everywhere silent bargains are struck—there is a code of signals made by fingers touching under the skirt of a robe. The shouts come after the affair has been concluded.

Over this life there floats a rancid, pungent odor, perfumed with incense and aromatic woods, the magnificent, unforgettable odor of the Orient.

The whites and Hindus hiding in their hygienic lairs work under the wings of fans, in offices where silent natives walk barefoot among the tables, and the typewriters endlessly inscribe a small number of little black signs. The life of the Europeans consists of combining these signs, breaking them down, and recombining them. It is a game for madmen. Outside, under the streaming sun, flocks of sheep go down to the docks, black heads, red heads, their broad, short tails full of fat.

In the great, open port between Steamer Point and Maala, there is tremendous activity. The liners of the P. and O. and the Messageries Maritimes clear a path for themselves through a tangle of peeling freighters, tankers, motor boats, and Arab *boutres*. The *boutres* are like caravels, with beautiful blue or green forecastles whose reflections crawl on the water like ser-

pents. When the liners are in port, the colonials go aboard—
the women head for the hairdresser's and the men for the bar.

The oil flows through big, jointed pipes that run just below
the surface of the water, like sea serpents—the only authentic
ones. The oil feeds the ships' tanks.

Not so long ago, Aden was a coaling station. Oil brought with
it offices, docks, the black tanks of the Anglo-Persian and Asiatic
Petroleum, and intrigues that rouse the emotions of the little
native potentates who have become sellers of oil and buyers of
gasoline for automobiles. A little war for concessions is spreading
all around. So Aden still conforms to its destiny. In Arabia the
smell of leather, and the smell of oil that grows more insolent
every month, are replacing the smell of the coffee from Sana and
Harar. But this change of products has not changed the human
consequences. One reads in Reclus: "To extend coffee plantations, European wars have been undertaken, vast territories have
been conquered in the New World, in Africa, and in the Sunda
Islands; millions of slaves have been captured and transported to
the new plantations; a revolution has been accomplished, entail-
ing consequences incalculable in their complexity, in which good
and evil are intermingled, in which frauds, warfare, oppression,
wholesale massacres go hand in hand with commercial enterprise. . . ."

The warehouses of Maala and Somalipura are stacked up to
their roofs of corrugated iron with sacks of sugar and rice, bales
of leather and goat hides, and cases of oil stamped with a bear or
gazelle. The Arab laborers sing at their work in these roasting
sweat-boxes; without the rhythm of work songs they would forget
what to do.

The wisdom of nations approves of all this scheming and
contracting and forcing, all this profitable slavery. But what says
the Wisdom that does not belong to nations?

What a strange idea, to have taken root on this rock. Everywhere else human beings cling to places where there is water surrounded by trees and fields that can be irrigated. But in this
country without springs they drink the scanty rainwater and

water distilled from the Indian Ocean. Ships bring back cargos of water drawn from the canal that supplies fresh water to Suez. Sometimes there is a storm at night, and the inhabitants, drunk with sleep, get up to watch as if it were a procession. The storm fills up "Cleopatra's Cisterns," deep tanks that are more mysterious than the catacombs.

Men are made for anchorages. Everywhere else in the world that is wisdom on their part; here it is a black and willful madness. They are always ready to set out on the longest routes around their globe, but no sooner do they reach a port than they fasten onto the smallest heap of sand. These drillers of walls bore holes in the rock for obscure purposes. In Aden you call these purposes war, commerce, and transit: do you think these words will excuse everything until the end of time?

VIII

In this mixture of the Orient and the British Empire, I felt a surprising vertigo that I had not anticipated and that accelerated from week to week, from one evening to the next.

It was the same vertigo experienced by men who have destroyed their habits and who have not lost everything in that Pyrrhic victory.

I became aware that I had no habits, that I was clean. I had habits of translating, of trying to figure things out by logical analysis—a few customs of the intellect. But when it came to action, I did not have the crutch of habit to lean on. The only groups to which I had belonged were familial and academic, and that was of no use whatever to a young man suddenly thrust into the midst of the evil world of adults and a lot of talk about oil.

I sought in vain for any obligations I might have, for some of those habits that no one understands, those imaginary gods whose shadow falls across every man's heart.

I belonged to no tribe, I was bound by no chains, yet here I was in the midst of crowds where every passerby recognized his own kind and could respond with the correct ritual, the correct password and countersign.

These automatic exchanges provide men with an illusion of happiness, with illusions about life, defeat, peace, and war. This keeps them from the sudden realization that they are walking through their existence like dogs through a game of ninepins.

For me there was nothing prescribed and nothing forbidden, neither meat, nor wine, nor clothing, nor women of a particular caste, nor modesty, nor debauchery. No one to worship, to move with prayers, to thank with offerings. In this absence of gods and angels, I was stripped of the symbols of piety, stripped of laws, catechisms, cults, and slogans. Acts seemed no more moral to me than the movement of the leaves on a tree. I lived in the midst of nature; men, animals, and objects were part of nature, they were not transfigured. A vulture was a vulture, a cow was a cow, the flag over the French Consulate was a piece of cloth. I did not have to wear my hair in the shape of a cow's hoof or covered by a turban as long as a shroud. It is necessary to understand that a cork helmet does not conciliate any people or divinity, and that a white linen suit is simply a suit that absorbs the least rays. The colonial European does not perceive what wide horizons would be opened to him if he only understood the nature of his jackets, which are machine-made and purely functional.

In short, I floated through a sea of regulations, codes, and religious machinations like a fish through water.

The others lived by clans, religions, skin colors, and nations, by clubs, business houses, and regiments. They spent their time inventing subdivisions, partitions, and steps on which to climb up and down like monkeys. They looked at each other like enemy units on campaign. To think that these madmen could have loved other human beings, that that was what they were made for! The Arabs hated the Jews, and the members of the Union Club despised the members of the International Club, which admitted Italian engineers from the salt works and Greek cigarette manufacturers whom no officer of the British artillery could mention without a sneer.

There was an inextricable maze of social distinctions through which all these people glided, finding their way with marvelous dexterity. On the lowest steps of the hierarchy stood the humble, dirty Jews, who lived clustered around the synagogue where they sought consolation for many an insult by praying to the god of vengeance, their shoulders covered by prayer-shawls as poetic as the night. At the top of the pyramid stood the agent of the Peninsular, two or three businessmen who were powerful along the Red Sea, the officers, the governor, and, in the Crescent at Steamer Point, the seated statue of the fat queen Victoria, with pendulous cheeks and the little, pinched eyes of a drunkard.

One understands many things if one knows that each of these men was destined to be buried according to the rites of his tribe, with every possible kind of prayer—Catholic, Jewish, Puritan, Presbyterian, Methodist, Parsee, Jainist, Moslem. There were dead men who were laid on a bed of rock, others who were burned, others who were abandoned to the grilling of the sun and the curved beaks of vultures. No dead man disappeared in a really reasonable way, into a true nothingness, providing no pretext for a rite.

IX

He is one of the pistons of the huge machine called commerce.

—Balzac, *Modeste Mignon*

From here I can see Aidrus Road climbing toward the great green and white mosque Aidrus, from the top of which early in the morning the priest cries the prayer to the four winds of the horizon, while other mosques answer from the four corners of Crater.* The goats lying in doorways, the natives lying on their beds of cord like dead men dressed in white, stir a little. The road comes to an end, divided by spurs of rock, and loses itself in paths that lead into the mountain toward the bays, the quarries, the slaughterhouses, and the Tower of Silence, house of the dead.

There are crowds of passers-by, people celebrating, and those yelping Arab funeral processions whose members trot like walking champions. All day long the coolies run through the debris-laden dust, dragging wagons loaded with dried hides and chanting their wordless work song. Tall Somali girls pass, holding an edge of their holy virgins' veils between their teeth and laughing to the men with their eyes. The Indian girls offer strong bare arms and brown, elastic surfaces of flesh between their skirts and the tight blouses bound around their shoulder blades and breasts. The two American girls of Aidrus Road walk with a gazelle at their heels. All men and all women are strangers to me.

From a deep interior court rises the smell of hides cured under the sun of the high Abyssinian plateaus or on the stony ground of the Somalilands, in those countries whose names would fire the imagination of a child sitting on his bench in primary school: Berbera, Ogaden, Danakil, Harar, Mogadiscio, Addis Ababa.

A sound like melted butter sputtering in a pan, made by coffee

---

* The main urban division of Aden and the oldest section of the city, located in the two-mile crater of an old volcano. (Trans.)

beans on the screens of separators, forms a background for all other sounds.

Here, in a house built of black blocks, a house that wields more power between Suez and Kenya than any European ministry, is the chief of a great company, with his directors and troops of women and clerks whose heads are spinning because they are so far from London, from the Elephant and Castle tramway, from the meager gardens of their suburbs, from the electric trains that roll toward Cannon Street and London Bridge between eight and nine in the morning. People like all the children of Europe.

The chief is one of those men of such vast power that people who know him cannot fall asleep at night without a thought of him lurking at the back of their minds.

He possesses what three-quarters of the individuals most liberally endowed with a sense of their own importance do not have: cable addresses in Bombay, New York, Marseille, and London, and a private cable code. His red and green pennant floats over ships carrying his merchandise. His will appears to weigh upon the future of the tanneries and the international trade in leather gloves. Agents rule in his name in the Red Sea ports and in the medieval market towns of Abyssinia. His name is a password as far as Sana in Yemen and the frontiers of Shoa. He speaks arrogantly to the native sultans who live in the oases of the interior and the states of Hadhramaut.

There are false men of action—he is one of them. He tells you: "I have always lived totally, my life is an uninterrupted series of actions, of battles waged and won. This country to which I came more than twenty years ago, poor and proud, bears the scars of my action. It bears witness for me. It knows me." Thus he lies to you and to himself.

Not one of those acts has added anything to the poor man that he was then and still is. He is incomplete, like an abandoned construction job behind a fence covered with gaudy advertisements. Are we to take the reflections of action for action itself? Each of us is divided among the men he might be, and Mr. C. has allowed to triumph within him that man for whom life consists of making the price of coffee and Abyssinian leather go up or down on the market of Djibouti or Diredawa, the one who is a buyer and seller of little black signs. In the history of a sack of coffee you will find only a few actions: making a tree grow, drinking a cup of brew. Fighting abstract entities such as firms, unions, merchants' guilds—are you going to call that action? I want to fight a particular man, I want to hate a particular villainous face, this boss, such-and-such an attorney, this army major, that puritanical kill-joy. What have you to do with life, you with your imitations and your *trompe-l'oeil*—which count for nothing in the establishment of a flesh and blood existence, of justice, and of joy—you with your manufactured hatreds and angers and moments of weakness, your diminutions and your reflections in the water.

Here was a man of woman born who had performed all the motions of his life high in the regions of the abstract, in the firmament of discounts and exchanges, in the cruel sky that bends down over the heads of simple folk only to corrupt them and wither them like the little heads of Indian mummies. These motions formed a kind of icy garland around the memories of those who had known him. The past in which he took such excessive pride could all be summed up in the number of *lakhs* of rupees he had to his credit at the National Bank of India.

While he thought he was acting and planning his moves to suit himself, in reality he was subject to forces whose power was not derived from him and whose sources, if he had bothered to look for them, might have seemed mysterious and charged with a meaning that was ultimately revolting.

To handle rates of foreign exchange, to hover over the value of the thaler and the pound as if it were the temperature curve of a sick child, to make a ship move faster in order to secure a cargo—these empty dreams constituted his idea of action, on days when he didn't have to charm anyone.

He thought about his freedom and talked about it as if he were deluded by the feelings he had inspired in lesser men: the envy and respect of those who told him sincerely that he was free.

But the jellyfish thinks it is free, bankers and merchants think they are free. They too are mad, they are no better than the travelers. Seated behind their desks adorned with a Bentley Code and a Broomhall (the employees, attentive as soldiers, are standing on the other side of the desk), they put on knowing airs, they dictate, they reflect—forgetting that the dictation and the clever maneuvers originated far away and have reached them by way of ten coded telegrams, and letters that have traveled a long distance. They understand nothing.

Mr. C. was merely the megaphone for innumerable sound waves which he faithfully echoed. One must not confuse a free man with a barometer, a phonograph, or a Morin machine.* What untold sorrow this confusion can cause when the machine records not figures but political decisions or maxims of moral wisdom. What is most repugnant to me about my brothers is to see them living like worms: worms understand nothing about the force of gravity, nor men about their God, their desires, or their acts. Everything floats above their heads, and they think they have invented it all.

It did not take great genius, or the great enthusiasm he thought he felt, to be a sounding board for so many voices. Even the most musical echoes are not models of virtue. The reproduction of sounds—what name are we to give to this passive operation? Carried along in the round of trade and finance whose constantly accelerating movement no one could stop, he commanded slaves bound to the same wheel, slaves who were less sensitive echoes and needed first to hear the sound of his voice.

Fortunately, he was not at peace. He was surrounded, as it were, by an atmosphere of deadly foreboding that prevented him from greeting each new day with joy. He was waiting for something terrible to happen, he did not believe in his own plans. No respite, no moment of relaxation. The suction pump that was draining his life continued to go up and down with inexorable regularity. With increasing frequency he even talked about

---

* A mechanical device for demonstrating the laws of gravity by means of a graph traced on a rotating cylinder by a falling metal weight. (Trans.)

abandoning everything one day, leaving his stocks of leather, his reserves of gasoline, his stacks of ledgers and his filing cabinets. But these substances, these ledgers, had become *his* substance: to flee would have been the death of him.

Supposing someone had denounced him? Supposing someone had called him to account, in the name of all the men who had been drained in his service, men who had become trembling, obsequious mannikins. In the name of his own children whom he had crushed.

He would have answered that his heart was pure. Every murderer washes his hands afterward. He would have expatiated on the greatness of his works: ten million hides of every category shipped per year, trading posts marking the borders of a realm, events set in motion at a distance, in Grenoble, in Mazamet, four ships at sea. A fine total to tip the scales in a man's favor. I see Mazamet huddled at the foot of the Black Mountain, with its watered meadows, its garages, its record number of automobiles per thousand inhabitants, its billion business transactions per year, the smiles on the faces of its innkeepers, and its black suburbs full of men who wash hides for a living. I see the glove workers of Millau, the bent backs of the shopgirls at Perrin's, the Somali laborers torn from their villages and their flocks to be insulted by all the whites of Djibouti.

Mr. C. was not absolutely immune to the gnawing of the inner life. One can imagine that Ford has dreams, that Poincaré invents universes for himself when he is tired of falsifying diplomatic documents and inaugurating monuments to the dead.

This master of a great company faithfully preserved vestiges of a sentimental adolescence that had been troubled by a taste for fame and a kind of poetic ambition. He sought the conversation of women and liked them to play him pieces by Chopin that fit in with a traditional view of love. Sometimes he made pilgrimages to Stratford or Bayreuth. He would hold his head in his hands while he listened to Siegfried, or thought about the Hermaphrodite from the baths of Diocletian or the stained glass windows of Saint-Nazaire de Carcassonne. He would forget the columns of his accounts and turn to books, hoping to find in fiction everything that remained neglected on the edges of his life. Although his entire existence belied such a judgment, he was one of those men who build retreats for themselves out of the carefully accumulated debris of time. It really pained him not to be a man, and he tried to create a solitary image of one. So there were times when he was vulnerable. But what a spectacle it was to see him come back to the present of the business world, throwing off his dreams like a man who wakes up at will. It was as if he used these periods of rest to regroup his forces in deep retreats; he would reappear harder and better armed against men. He would become once more the pitiless phantom that his real existence had substituted for the man he might have been. Moreover, I have seen him use the elements of his dreams to attract certain persons to himself and to the service of his profits. There were some young men who offered less resistance to a man who looked as if he were capable of feeling—a man with whom they might reasonably hope to have human relations—than to the deadly formulas of business conversations and employment contracts. He let a few of his employees catch glimpses of a life of the mind, the pleasures of conversation, and the sovereign good of business ethics and standards of conduct. These young men proved conciliatory regarding the level of their wages.

He suggested that I make my flight from Europe permanent by settling in Aden, and offered for my mature years a power that would have differed from his own only in degree. This is it: if you flee, if your flight succeeds in the sense that worldly men understand success, you will be Mr. C. You will be Mr. C. everywhere. It is the last offer you will get. But give up the idea of being a man.

I had discovered another life that was almost a perfect counterpart to the life of Mr. C. On the Esplanade in Crater, near Palonjee Dinshaw's, stood a shop that was a kind of museum. It contained a few pieces of flotsam and jetsam left by the passage of men—coins, monuments, inscriptions whose secrets one would have liked to penetrate, like the secrets of the youthful adventures of one's father. Just looking at them, you thought, as Napoleon had, of Ophir. For the rest, it was like being at Bouvard and Pécuchet's. The curator of the museum had been a sergeant in the British army. Forty years of Aden. He had sunk so low, in the eyes of the English, as to smoke the native cigarettes, wear a *foutah,* and work as a public scribe for the Arabs. He would sit in front of his door and watch an inexhaustible little stream of boredom trickle by. He no longer knew anyone in his old county who bore his name. No point in going to visit trees under which you will see no familiar faces. He got drunk every night, fearing madness and protecting himself from its attacks with alcohol. He was like a red stone, lying outside the main currents in which nearly everyone managed to swim. None of the Europeans knew that an Englishman had come to rest there—or rather, that this drowning had taken place. The military authorities had refused him the right to take part in the comical little Anglo-Turkish war around Aden, and he had never gotten over it; to him their refusal had meant that he was weak. The desire to fire stray bullets in the direction of the Turkish outposts had been his last dream of action. He was losing his memories without a struggle, like an old crow losing its feathers: such is the ultimate fruit of the love of travel. It is easy to discover the keys to these two existences that were so similar, so equally removed from human life. There is no point in looking for secrets that combine destinies when there are no secrets to be found.

All the people clinging to Mr. C. like pilot fish to their shark were dying the same death as he.

What is one to do among these people? What is one to do with the young Englishwomen? They have eyes of glass that look so real one can be led to believe that the pupils see. Then one day one exclaims, "It's alive," like the good people in front of the *Squatting Scribe* in the Louvre on Sunday.

What is one to do with the English officers and government officials, with their adventures in the hierarchy? They wear the colors of their regiment or school like decorations. There would not be the slightest possibility of their getting lost if they went around the world in any direction, on any meridian. Chances are someone would recognize them, even among the barbarians, at the North Pole, or in Spain. To them, the other countries inhabited by men are strange objects—planets, as it were, outside the orbit of the Empire, which has occasionally entered into contact with them, at Crécy, at Waterloo, on the Somme. They believe that empire is peace, and that on Judgment Day the eyes of Margaret Bannerman and the records of Lord Burghley will compensate for the tall, deadly houses of Edinburgh, for the coal strikes, and even for the existence of Sir Henri Deterding.* They are guided by ignorance, patriotic proverbs, a respect for oil and good table manners, and by romantic poetry.

There were the Indians, the Arabs, the impenetrable Blacks. I could not afford to spend ten years settling down among them and getting to know them. All things considered, I would live among the Europeans. It is the masters of men whom one must fight and overthrow. Time enough to make fine friends when the war is over.

---

* Margaret Gordon, later Lady Bannerman (1798–1878): Thomas Carlyle's first love, a beautiful young Canadian whom he immortalized as Blumine in *Sartor Resartus*. Lord David Burghley (1905–   ): a celebrated English athlete, an Olympic hurdling champion. Sir Henri Deterding (1866–1939): a Dutch oil magnate and honorary Knight of the British Empire who, as director-general of the Royal Dutch-Shell group of companies, built a huge industrial empire and controlled a large part of the petroleum production of the world; in the 1930's he became a supporter of the Nazi movement in Germany. (Trans.)

X

*In the smallest towns of Italy one finds a theatre, music,
and extemporaneous poets; everywhere there is great
enthusiasm for poetry and the arts, and glorious sun-
light. In short, in Italy one feels he is alive.*

—Madame de Staël, *Corinne*

Once the novelty of people and places has worn off, when the
colors have become ordinary and the scenes less striking, it is
possible to try to understand Aden.

Aden is a knot that ties many strands together. It did not
take me many months to exhaust the picturesque sights and
sounds of the Orient and to recognize the forces that pulled
the strings and drew the knot tight. Aden is a crossroads of
several sea routes staked out by lighthouses and little islands
bristling with cannon; it is one of the links in the long chain
that maintains the profits of London businessmen around the
world. A port of call full of murderous symbols, a companion
piece to Gibraltar.

It was just the time when the European armies were lending
their soldiers to help civilize the Chinese. A badly run economy
begins by straightening out the affairs of other countries.

There was promise of a revolution around the river mouths
of Kwangtung Province, so ships were moving toward Asia. The
troop transports, the destroyers with their sharks' snouts cast
anchor opposite the gothic Customs building, the crews took
the air in the evening on the runways of the aircraft carriers. In
Aden, the batallions swarmed out of their barracks like wasps
from a nest, and silence took up winter quarters at the club of
the Second Devon Regiment, which I could see from my window. No more band nights when the orchestra played *God Save
the King* and the *Marseillaise*, awaking docile and ignoble echoes
in the hearts of coffee and oil merchants. One read the dispatches
of the Eastern Telegraph Company to get news of China.

These everyday details will perhaps suffice to indicate the range of the life men lived in Aden.

This is what one had to understand: Aden was a highly concentrated image of our mother Europe, it was Europe compressed. A few hundred Europeans huddled together in a space as cramped as a prison ship, five miles long by three miles wide, reproduced on a small scale, but with extraordinary precision, the designs formed by the lines and relationships of life in the western countries. The Orient reproduces the Occident and is a commentary on it.

You see before you a sort of diagram that is a faithful representation of the original, like the portolanos of the Renaissance or the symbolic designs patiently composed by the monks in Buddhist monasteries. The liquid has been decanted and only the essence is left; everything that diluted the solution has evaporated.

There remains a dry, pitiless residue that can be described.

In Aden only a small number of men are caught up in the driving belts of this complex machine, and that is why it is possible to understand it; in Europe the meaning of existence is often hidden by the multitude of actors and the crisscrossing of their lives. To understand the laws of this machine and the source of its driving power seems really important to a young man who, having seen a bit of the world, has caught a first, tentative glimpse of the goal that men alone can strive for. The people of Aden play out their roles in little anecdotal dramas which, like shadow-plays, represent the characteristic pattern of life of civilized men. These roles are determined by habits and half-awakened passions, and by that simple set of drearily accepted customs: life. One can see here the validity of the Stoics' comparison with the theatre, even though it is necessary to shed further light on their thinking.

The inhabitants of Aden are no different from those of London and Paris. They are the same plants, but in a hothouse that makes them grow large. Like the people of Europe, they appear, pause, walk, weep, disappear, are eclipsed without rhyme or reason. At first you do not perceive the purpose of the entrances and exits, the bells ringing behind closed doors, the conversations. You simply guess that unknown plans and forces lie behind the visible activity and provide the keys to it. It is as if you were a child watching the grown-ups move about. You observe their existence, you can easily imitate their movements in order to try to understand them. But you soon realize that those movements are performed so reluctantly that you can never expect to get a single atom of contentment or joy out of them.

At last you penetrate this abstract performance in which the bit players are hardly more than two-dimensional. It is not difficult to understand, although the meaning of the drama is a collection of all the misconceptions about life.

These men were replaceable parts of an invisible mechanism that slowed down on Sunday, because of religion, and was periodically jammed by the violent accidents of economic crises. This whole mass of machinery, bolted together, without safety valves, vibrated like a structure of sheet iron. In every city in the world there are men watching and waiting for the day when the cover will blow off and the steam will explode.

Grouped under names of firms, they were perpetual victims of the warlike ritual of international trade. They reminded you of black savages who dance until they drop, in the night filled with spirits and reflections.

Like Emmanuel Kant, they were victims of that horrible arrangement, a daily routine. But unlike Kant, they had not invented their own routine. Kant at least had a way out—there was no one to prevent him from making up another one, or seven different ones a week, if he felt like it.

Six o'clock: get up, shower. Seven o'clock: breakfast. Eight o'clock: office. Twelve o'clock: lunch. One o'clock: siesta. Two o'clock: office. Five o'clock: stroll, club. Seven-thirty: dinner. Ten o'clock: bed.

That's the sort of schedule you find posted in the office of a colonel, or the vice-principal of a lycée, or a prison director. Since this little picnic lasted two summers and three winters for each of them, after allowing for sleep and the office, where were they going to find time and leisure to be men? They didn't even have movies on Saturday night. They were running under the blows of a whip they had never seen.

One can understand that there are more methodical arguments in favor of the revolution, but few that are more persuasive than this one: it takes leisure to be a man. This argument is found even in that old slave-driver Plato.

Every second of time that they passed—or rather, that passed them by—was subject to the pressure of the world market. Everywhere men are subject to that pressure and that pressure only. But by the time it reaches them it has been diverted into so many channels, so many pipes where its force appears to dissipate like steam, that they retain the illusion that they are independent and even autonomous. In Aden, this pressure was an immediate presence, there were no intermediaries. It must be understood that in Aden life was free of the false adornments that bygone centuries of moral civilization have added to it in Europe, free of the illusions and hypocrisies that are necessary where there is social struggle. These people expected to go back to their native country one day. So they were patient, and reserved the use of illusions for the time of their return. They were sure they would have them when they needed them. They thought their lives would be unhappy only for a time. The Arab and Somali workers were still submissive enough so that it was unnecessary to invent arguments that would justify to the world their methodical exploitation. Those arguments were kept for the workers of Europe. Since illusions seemed superfluous, the people of Aden did not devote to them the few moments of respite their busy days afforded. There was no news except what came in cables from the agencies; no one needed the European newspapers or felt the courage to read them: they piled up unopened in the corners of bedrooms. No theatres, no publishing houses, no libraries except for the English grammars, the arithmetics, and the pious books of the missions. No speeches, no philosophy, all the décor was forgotten and temporarily abolished. No leisure for idleness, no leisure for love. In this stifling hole where people were obliged to live elbow to elbow—there were 580 inhabitants per square mile—there was not one of those solitary places where lovers can be sure they will not be observed. Besides, there was only one woman for every three males. No music, no traveling fairs. And what white man would have been admitted to a feast in honor of Ramadan, or to that strange Hindu carnival at which the gravest of old men sprinkle themselves with ink, and austere doors are decorated with obscene symbols?

When you tried to talk about fine arts and social questions, your words rang so false and hollow that every voice fell silent. You felt it was pointless to take these disguises seriously, they seemed as out of place as obscenities at the bishop's table.

Since man's life was reduced to a state of absolute purity—the economic state—you were never in danger of being deceived by the distorting mirrors that reflect life in Europe. Since art, philosophy, and politics were absent because they served no purpose, you did not have to make any correction for them. You could see the foundations of western life, men were stripped naked like anatomical models: for the first time I saw people who did not require a philosophy of clothes.

No concession to the love of art, nothing to sing, nothing to venture, nothing to paint, no poems to read or write. The only genuine events of their days were the cables from the Eastern Telegraph Company, anonymous instruments of the powers let loose upon the markets of Europe and the United States. Every heart hung on the electric waves that traveled under mountains of sea at a rate of speed which no shareholder of Shell tried to imagine. These men who on Sunday morning opened the mail brought by the India pouch were anchored there in order to make more money than they would have made at home, in their English counties or their French prefectures; that is, in order to secure for their later years and their old age the privilege of waiting for death without doing anything, except perhaps a little gardening or golf. What petty bourgeois these colonial rulers were at heart.

At five o'clock in the afternoon, since they lived at a cadence set by the sun, they would come out of their shelters and try to imagine that somewhere in the world there were rivers. All day long in Aden, in the center of the white sky, there is the presence of the sun. Rocks split open, in a single moment of carelessness a man can be struck down, but toward the end of the day the sun moves toward the semaphore station of Shamshan. A sort of armistice is concluded, and half the streets are liberated. The shadows grow long like the stems of plants in the depths of a ravine, the fans make a few final turns like a propeller after the plane has landed.

Then they abandon the filing cabinets in which the contracts sleep, the drawers full of bills of lading, statute books, and copies of letters.

Around the soccer field in Crater, on the Esplanade, would be assembled Arabs from Hadhramaut and Yemen, Indians of every caste, and Blacks from the African coast, mixed with His Majesty's infantry. Sometimes the Punjabi regimental band would be playing. On sabbath days the young Jews would be learning the ways of the world, not yet daring to shave their ritual locks but only to wear the light-colored jackets that they would one day put on for good on the sidewalks of Mohammed Ali Square, at the entrance to the Bazaar in Cairo.

In front of the Presbyterian chapel some artillerymen and a few young Indians would be practicing cricket. The priests from the Italian mission would pass near them, dressed in white linen cassocks and heavy black shoes such as police inspectors wear— inspectors of moral intentions, prosecutors of the confessional.

Cars would be leaving for the places where there was water, the garden in Sheik Othman's oasis, Fisherman's Bay, and the Gold-Mohur Club where the white women of the colony swam. A few couples would be going up to the isolated lighthouse of Ras Marshag.

People would be going to the crevasses in the walls of the volcano to see a few trees swollen with water like cabbages and bearing flowers that looked like apple blossoms or, on days after one of those pathetic rainstorms, to see meadows of white lilies. Or they would be going up above the cisterns to see an exiled Hindu who let flocks of short-legged swifts nest among his effects.

Billiards would be resounding in the clubs, people would be drinking or playing cards and listening to dance music at Steamer Point. These were their meager hours of truce. At this time they tried to do something for their bodies. Fortunately, most of them were English so they knew how to go about it. Their bodies came to life for one or two hours, but not the Italian bodies or the French bodies. Too prudent to move.

This was also the time when they did give in to illusions after all. Like Mr. C., they talked about action. That is a word which sets all men to dreaming, it is the thing they do not have. They tried to make themselves believe that they were acting, and in the end they did believe it. They were therefore poetic: to be poetic is to need illusions. They developed this illusion with all the resources of the intelligence, their old servant-mistress: they made up a theory about it.

But no one was deceived. You could tell they did not love their life. It was no good for them to work at it, love would not come. They went on living, thinking about what they had done, about what they had to do, time passed. It was nervous habit that kept them going. They were well trained; their parents could be proud of them, and their bosses too. They didn't look human, they were more like empty sacks. If you had cut open their stomachs—that was the only favor you could have done them—a little dust would have flowed out. They boasted of having possessed women, of having been wounded in war, yet you could not imagine living liquids like semen or blood coming out of them.

The objects of their desire did not exist. The things that were important to them were abstractions. You could not even personify them so as to work them into a figure of speech: the balance of an account, a schedule of assets and liabilities, credit, the circulation of capital, business success, professional duty. Can you go to bed with capital? These entities kept them busy, filling up their minutes, stealing all the time around them. The people themselves were abstract. They carried out all the instructions that do not concern men as though they were obeying the secret commands of some incurable vice. Nevertheless, they said "life"; despite everything, they thought "let us live." First cry on awakening, last sigh before turning out the light. But in order to live they would have had to be cured of their bad habits, their digestion, their respiration, their marriages, their hand-writing, their languages. To be transformed from the ground up. But they were men obsessed, and they were dying by inches in the service of anonymous capital.

The awful thing was to watch them sleep. They slept at night, and they slept after meals like snakes digesting. I would see them under the galleries of the house, sleeping in their wicker armchairs. At last they were at rest, they had arrived at a friendly port, a safe harbor, at the only happiness of the day, unlaced, unwound, with one cheek resting on a shoulder, their necks creased, hands trailing, drops of sweat rolling down their foreheads. Their open faces would be crossed by waves of visible dreams, the last heaves of the ground swell that rose from the depths of their humanity and lifted them the way insects lift dead animals lying in ditches. They would make a humming sound and change position. They would try to remember the treasures they had found in sleep, so as to carry them over into the waking state. But they could not hold on to them, they would come back empty-handed, more sorrowful than a woman with a stillborn child. For a living man sleep is the state of detachment that is most like death; for them it was the very peak of attention, their most extreme effort, it was all they would ever know of what a living man desires.

How many times will I have repeated the word "man." But what other word is there? That's what it is all about: to say what is, and what is not, in the word "man."

What is to be done with these creatures made of glass whose very daydreams are visible? They are crystal madmen out of Edgar Allan Poe. But glass can be broken. Or you might compare them to the transparent fish of the great sea depths. But fish can be caught.

Because there are many of them, stuck one on top of the other, at first you think they have substance. When there are many transparent layers together, they seem opaque. Such is the description of mica. You have only to find the planes of cleavage, then each flake, each separate man, is transparent.

I was always allowed to believe that men did have substance. Now I find there is something which prevents them from being like real men, like the men mentioned in history, for example, or in poetry. Will man never be anything but a historical figure?

XI

When you want a change, you can go inland to Lahej, or by boat to Djibouti.

If you go to Lahej, it's to see some grass.

The cars pitch their way through the desert, getting a running start from a distance in order to climb the hills of sand that grab at the wheels like suction cups. When you come to a resting place you see the Arabs feeding leaves to their kneeling camels. You pass near a mound of potsherds that is supposed to bear witness to the passage of Albuquerque in 1519.* After several hours trees rise and you come in sight of Lahej, a city of dust with houses of dust, palm trees of dust, men of dust.

The sultan's palace is a building of gray coral. It has a balustraded roof, rows of windows, pilasters, Corinthian columns. In the garden bunches of tobacco leaves are strung up to dry. There are balls of frosted glass to read the future in, such as you find in the suburbs of Paris.

You enter. At the top of a bare staircase, a tall Arab in a red-and-yellow striped silk jacket asks you to wait in the audience chamber. It is a large drawing room in semi-darkness, the shutters closed against the sun. The walls are hung with life-size color photographs of the father and uncle of the reigning sultan. The rugs, which come from Paris, lie in a corner rolled up and tied, as if the sultan were at the seaside, or as if he were giving a little hop that evening in honor of the eighteenth birthday of his son, who has steel-rimmed glasses and pimples like a student at the École Normale de Saint-Cloud. You drink spiced coffee out of those imitation china cups that Armenians and Syrians sell on the deck of liners that put into port from the Far East. You sit on velvet settees in the style of Napoléon III— on the edge of the seat, respectfully: he's a reigning prince.

---

* Actually, it was in 1513 that Albuquerque besieged Aden. He died in 1515. (Trans.)

Comes the said prince, a tall black man with the crafty, cruel look of gangsters around the old port in Marseille. The conversation doesn't compromise anyone: he is not about to tell you what he thinks of the Wahabites or the Imam of Sana. Finally you are authorized to wander about freely on the territory of Sir Abdul Karim, Knight Commander of the Bath, who withdraws.

Then you go look at the grass. The road, running parallel to the little railroad from Lahej to Aden, is bordered with stone walls covered with dry clods, as in Brittany.

You enter an area full of date trees, guava trees, papayas, orange trees, and pomegranates. You cross fields of Chinese banana trees no taller than a boy of fifteen. The earth is a carpet of damp felt made of fleshy plants. Canals run around the fields between raised banks, as in the Nile delta. They are filled with running water. In the background you see the mountains of Yemen again, bigger now. Suddenly, at the bottom of a red ravine broader than the valley of the Loire, there flows the trickle of a half-dead river.

What joy! Here are meadows with grass like the grass in Burgundy, fields with all the colors of a field in Piedmont. The most formal visitors stretch out on the grass, almost trembling, after weeks of stones, at the sight of peasants and fresh water in locks, as in the *Georgics*. They lean over the wheel of a well. Unfortunately, someone's foot turns over the white corpse of a snake. During lunch under the lemon trees, eagles steal the bones people throw to the dogs, plummeting from the sky and leaving the dogs to snap their jaws on empty air and a stray feather.. This is not the peaceful countryside of the Occident; it is not Tuscany, Touraine, or Kent.

On the roads you meet bands of workers coming in from the fields. They are naked except for a *foutah* held round the waist by a belt of embroidered leather from which hangs a curved knife in a silver sheath. They have a heavy black wire around one ankle. A leper sitting by the side of the road brushes away the evening flies with a slow, mechanical gesture.

It would be impossible to find men more ruined than the sultan's subjects. Compared to them, the laborers I once saw coming out of the bauxite mines on the road to Aix-en-Provence, their bodies covered with red earth, breathed forth strength and joy. Twenty thousand human beings lead a life of purgatory so that this native Marquis de Carabas* can watch his meadows turn green in the shadow of the military airplanes of the English, so that he can look at himself in peace in his globes of glass, and travel to Cairo, London, and Paris. On the way to Lahej you thought about the grass and about the women you would like to push down on it after several months of chastity, but now you find the grass is guilty too, as guilty as the smokestacks of the factories in Saint-Ouen.

Orient, under thy palm trees so dear to poets, again I find only more human misery.

Another day I leave for Djibouti on the motor boat *Halal*. The *Halal* is an old hand at plying the Red Sea. It is a vessel of about four hundred tons, weighed down by loading derricks, with a thin smokestack in the stern. Captain MacLean lets it run itself; it is not a capricious boat that you have to keep an eye on during every watch. It makes straight for the Somali coast on its own, like a farmer's horse heading for market with his master asleep on the cabbages.

MacLean sleeps, tells stories about women, and takes a drink from each of the calabashes hanging among the gear inside his cabin. At an appointed time he always changes his white suit and dons a sun helmet and a clean pair of shoes: the *Halal* is coming in sight of Djibouti. At the far end of the Bay of Tadjoura you can see the low coast of madrepore coral. In the background, as in a painting by da Vinci, there are blue tiers of mountains crowned with clouds, the beginning of Abyssinia.

---

* A character in a song of the same title written in 1816 by the popular poet Béranger to satirize certain elements of the nobility. His name has passed into the language meaning a reactionary old aristocrat of boundless pride and self-importance who has only contempt for the common people. (Trans.)

As soon as the ship has dropped anchor, the lighters arrive, loaded with bales of leather. Shouting Somali oarsmen with glistening skin begin to dance a wild and weightless ballet around the ship's hull. They dive naked, catch the end of a line between their teeth, climb up by the anchor chain, and leave their long, wet footprints on the bridge. MacLean is already walking on the mole. He exchanges his bills of lading with the director of the trading post and heads straight for the cafés and the girls.

Djibouti has no past. It is a sub-prefecture of the South of France that was built forty years ago. It is just old enough for the pink wash of the houses to have begun to peel and for the trees in the governor's garden to have begun to look like trees.

The same life as in Aden, but in a rowdier atmosphere, amid the cries of southern Europe: Greek, French, Italian. In Aden there are closed clubs: you can never look through the windows and see what is happening inside. In Djibouti there are cafés, *belote* takes the place of bridge, and the men talk about women. What a surprise for a Frenchman to find here the details that make France France, the little things that make it wear, on the same body as England, other clothes. I feel at home on the Place Ménélik, sitting in a sidewalk café like the ones in Montélimar or Avignon, in front of a stand of hackney cabs with fringed awnings, as in Périgueux. I feel at home when I hear the superintendent of police standing at the door of the police station insult a native in the voice of a former sergeant-major of the colonial troops. I feel at home on the tennis courts, talking to the President of the Tribunal, who has a Radical-Socialist beard and a Gascon belly, and to his wife, who is cut on the same pattern as the colonels' wives in the metropolitan country and the matrons of the Rue Paradis. At home in front of the post office, wondering how the director managed to buy a car so fast. At home on the Plateau du Serpent when I see the young girls out walking with a bandeau around their hair like the ones they wear in Quiberon, and again when I learn who is sleeping with the wife of the railroad manager. At home, finally, when I discover at a Greek grocer's, under piles of canned tunafish from Amieux's, the Greek text of *Prometheus Bound* and *Oedipus at Colonus.*

The same formless boredom as in Aden, but in shirtsleeves held up by elastic bands that barbers wear, and with the taste of vermouth-cassis and tangerine-curaçao. All these men are going around in circles too, knocking against the invisible walls of their destiny, doing the same things at the same times as the English on the Asian coast, driving out in the evening to the experimental garden at Ambouli where couples go to console themselves, couples whose members are always interchangeable. It is night, you hold a nameless woman against you, the scrubby bushes of the steppe file by, and the camels graze on their tops. As these bushes have the shape and proportions of grown trees, you might think you were in a prehistoric landscape, with camels as big as iguanodons.

Since the French are in the habit of talking about love, even though they are no more susceptible to it than the English, Djibouti possesses a red-light district. In the native village, which the Somalis are forbidden to leave after ten o'clock at night without a *laissez-passer*, you look down streets that are like all the others, with heaps of fishbones, and poor reed huts that are swept away as soon as the river rises a little. They reek of rancid mutton fat overlaid with perfume.

You come to the end of these streets and the engine, throttled down, rumbles like an approaching storm in the listening silence. The girls come running from every door like madwomen delivered from the magic spell that kept them in the dark. They jump up and down in front of the radiator holding hands, shouting, and calling to each other in the shrill voices of singers. They are tall girls, very young, covered with big jewels. Their oiled skin gleams faintly in the headlights and in the red reflection of their huts. You feel hands on your neck like the paws of animals; you must leave or let yourself be sucked under, plunging into the waves of a love sunk deep in the steaming night. These descents are the last resort of lost men:

if you go into a black country, will you ever be able to forget its admirable little girls? But this perdition is still better than your dirty virtuous habits, people of Europe—you might as well go in for drug addiction or debauchery.

In the end, when it is time to return to the offices of Aden, one wonders whether it was really worth the trouble of leaving them.

XII

Although all the inhabitants of Aden are overburdened with work, there is absolutely nothing to do. That is the worst statement that can be made about men; it is an admission that they are condemned to a state of perpetual vacuity.

Not one crumb of reality, not one act that might lead to anything. A life of ineffectual boredom passed among companions who have grown accustomed over the years to everything that does not exist. Shadows begotten by all sorts of hungers: in time of famine, when there is no bread, men also have hallucinations. So what are you to do? Learn to live with boredom? Die this death? You have no alternative. Since you don't want to die yet—that would be like offending someone, like ignoring the most secret admonitions of life—you sink into boredom, too. You settle down among these performing animals who have nothing left to do except love each other with a hypocritical ardor that is really misplaced.

Now is the time of the descent into Hades. You have to pass through all the stages Ulysses went through, whether or not you are going to return to your native Ithaca. For each of us there is a region of sham thoughts, of ideas that are not really ideas, of living men who are dead. When everything in the external world seems to be forbidden to you, the inner life appears. That's all there is left. Now you can summon up your own shades with their everlasting twaddle and their prophecies.

I catch the fever—every vice has its germs. The fact that one has understood the nature and causes of an inhuman life is not enough to protect him against the sickness bred by that life. I live like a shade among other shades, everything moves with muffled footsteps among the stones of fever.

Nothing happens, there is no hurry about anything. I forget that I was once aware of the passage of time. If you feel that time is slipping by, you are living badly—but you are living.

When you live well, time does not slip by, it is possessed. I do not think about time any more: no one can foresee the day when it will start to move again.

Talk? To do that, you have to have something to say, and someone to talk to. I think I have extraordinary presentiments of what, to the jaded eyes of a living man, is the greatest boredom of all: death. I am no cleverer than anyone else. I simply cannot understand nothingness, *my* future nothingness, although the concept of nothingness clashes with the idea of its possession. So I see myself dead, but incompletely. I imagine a degraded form of existence—I haven't made much progress, it seems, since Achilles. In short, I take this state of boredom for a continual forewarning of death. It is horrible. Death disgusts me if that's all it really is, if it is not so much the negation of everything to come as a still-human weakness like sickness, cold, or physical pain. I feel as if I were already dead: indifference is ripe. I cannot call these weeks that I live through anything else but death; this is all a living man can think when he wants to come as close as he can to the meaning of nothingness. True death is what life is not. It is the state of a man when his mind is blank, when he is not aware of himself, when he does not think others are aware of him. I have not reached that point yet, nothing is lost, really. But the illusion of it is frightening.

I swaggered a bit in the beginning. I said to myself, I am reconciled with my body, I have been made over by the freedom of movement that solitude allows. But even a body can waste its time. It can spoil its chances of being united with the world of ideas. It must have objects for companions, or else it has nothing to do, it is all alone, it doesn't know what to do with its big muscles any more, it leaves the mind bankrupt. When it has forgotten the breath of the thin winds of Paris, the shifting of the sea breeze in the morning, the structure of frost, the plantations of salt and crystals protecting windowpanes, meadows, and rivers, when it has forgotten the corners of the world it was accustomed to, it is idle. In Aden my body has even less to do than in Paris. It can't find anything to occupy it. It has been set down on gray sands and volcanic pumice on the edge of coves frequented by rays, sharks, and rainbow-fish, as in the beginning of the world. The sea washes emaciated shores, skeletons of those creatures which in the Occident are called hills, promontories, and valleys. What can the body do with this glittering heap of broken minerals and, when night falls, with the company of Orion and the Southern Cross millions of light years away?

When the elements of the universe have been mysteriously decanted and nothing remains but colorless vapors and the dregs of tides and stones, I discover that my body is lost, I cannot use it, because there is no love, there are no human actions.

Then the mind begins to ruminate on the past and on the future, on what unknown possibilities the future may hold, on things that might have been but are no longer possible, on what was not, and on what yet may be. This life of idle speculation is the harvest of boredom. It is an existence in which no operation of the faculty of thinking, no real thought, ever takes place. Real thought concerns itself with the actual, which combines an immediate presence and some sort of activity: thought requires real objects that exist in a particular place at a particular time. It sets to work on them and summons up all its resources to do them honor. A thought wants something. It desires a concrete end.

When I go for a walk on the slopes of the volcano, I am all alone and wretched as a stone. I pass lava grottos full of bats, I walk along paths edged with rocks painted white, in the bottom of ravines where poison rue and thorn-bushes grow. Great, tireless vultures watch me from their nests. Night comes, like a cloud, or a bird. On the summit of Jebel Shamshan the sun goes down amid an icy solitude. This is the time of day when you can pick up pieces of lava without burning your fingers; they are flat stones in which the crystals make patterns that look like fossil ferns. I am lost. I want to return to men who are not waiting for me under the lights of Aden, men who are not there. The crater is a great urn in which the night piles up, accumulating the mysterious ingredients of its magic. The semaphore station exchanges its final signals with ships that still loom beyond the twin peaks of Little Aden, which sailors call the Ass's Ears. The darkness, cold as mercury, is full of invisible faces, of secret agreements, of drugs to be used for sympathetic magic. It beats like a heart. I am not saved from the pitiless day. I dare not hope for anything in this enormous night that spreads all around, cooling the deadly volcano surrounded by reflections of the moon in the sea.

I hardly want to think about this life that leads me. There is no material or human object in it; the love of a woman can be an object of thought, just as a tree can. All is absence. Show me my tools, my animals, my needs, my men. Show me fields, and weapons. If only I had a field everything would be all right, or if I had a real trade between my hands. I have objects that are my slaves. They are familiar but empty things, things that call for no invention or joy: furniture, penholders, taxis, teeth, eyeglasses, clothes, hands, doors.

We have to concern ourselves with objects. What a source of boredom and despair objects become when they are too familiar. They play as important a role in human lives as men do. It is a necessary act of charity to give them some thought.

Everyone has had the experience of coming upon strange apparitions. At Bourg-la-Reine, for instance, I once saw a melon that had grown inside a demi-john, a greater marvel than those four-masted schooners put in bottles by retired sailors sitting on the ramparts of Belle-Ile-en-Mer. Old-fashioned opticians sometimes decorate their windows with pieces of glass, tortoise shell, and metal. These objects are even less utilitarian than the poetic lenses displayed outside of pharmacies, prisms that cast colored lights over the sidewalk and transform everything they touch. Or one may suddenly see a white skull, pure as a celestial sphere, an old-fashioned atlas of the mind with the word "phrenology" tattooed on its forehead. Or again, the photographer's imagination may decorate his model's thighs with black lace and garters adorned with figurines, mottos and emblems which, like the pierced hearts of the Virgin of the Sorrows and the flowers of

Saint Theresa of Lisieux, divert the mind to the most unin-
habitable regions of love.

These liberated islands have lost all communication with the
incalculable quantities of matter fashioned for useful purposes.
No more bridges, no more handles. They have escaped from
the slavery of receptacles and instruments, and they cannot be
put to use in the ways that have been consecrated by the wisdom
of nations. For all their ugliness and poverty, we recognize them
as belonging to a world in which objects and their masters live
at liberty. Despite the fact that they were conceived by retired
civil servants, we can identify them with the drawings of
Leonardo da Vinci and the poems of Rimbaud; it is simply that
they have been so diverted from their true destiny that they have
sunk to the level of a cannon or a flag. They enable us to enter
a universe in which things do not require special directions for
use, where the actions corresponding to them do not have to be
learned, evoke no disgust, require no prophylactic measures, and
are subject to no sanctions. Unfortunately, by the age of twelve,
men already know by heart their entire retinue of objects. We
must search for objects which do not require special training
on our part, which do not call for actions standardized by the
bureau of weights and measures. A life filled with new objects,
objects capable of awakening everything in man that has never
yet been put to use, would be more joyous than anything conceived by Plato. Everything is to be hoped for from such a life.
All man's resources would be utilized—the resources of his body,
his instincts, his artistic abilities. We would become aware of
the existence of humanity. In the meantime, let us live in our
poverty, subject to habits imposed by objects, the manias of our
brothers: no one is happy. And yet our brothers can be the
simplest and most varied of our things.

In Aden this idleness is terrible, one is deprived of everything,
even of the semblance of art and philosophy.

So life is reduced to the shallowness of the past and the dust
of a future made up of habits and systems, the madness that
combines the elements of poverty and excludes melons in

bottles, seasons in hell, and free women. A chess match in which the living lose to the dead. The obscure foreboding that the number of these poverty-stricken combinations is infinite, leads to what can only be called despair. All the myths about the great void are simply descriptions of life lived in accordance with the intelligence and the old philosophy. The inner life is Intelligent. Despair flatters itself sometimes with being very subtle. The intelligence is an old madwoman who grinds up refuse and manufactures new things out of it. She arranges equal matches, in which opposing thoughts are always equally significant and attractive. The fact that she always regards them in an identical manner reduces them to this equality. She has two mottos: A is the same as B; it's all the same to me. Truth comes out of the mouths of puns. She busies herself even when her master finds nothing to do, because she must always keep going: what a life! Her master watches her function the way a paralytic watches his arm jump and tremble. There is no reason why it should stop. The master wants nothing, so he never comes upon an object which his intelligence tells him is really important and capable of displacing all other objects. For her, to encounter this thought or that is a matter of indifference, she is too pure to indicate a choice. She is a mirror that has no preference among the objects reflected, she is the locus of every thought possible. She doesn't give a rap about anything: she is just as happy performing analytical operations as she would be working out various possible worlds and possible lives for man. The only dream she can bear is algebra of one kind or another. The algebra of Leibnitz, for example, sets forth all the formulas for the inner life, everything that justifies the degradation of the outer life. She makes no proposals, she has no taste for anything: she invades the entire being, and from the inevitable failure of reason, the man who is gnawed by intelligence finally infers the universal defeat of mankind. This generalization is the ultimate limit of reason and its most perfect operation. There is nothing left to do but go on as before and think about death in a new way. When no aspect of life seems to offer any reason to make a choice, some men invent comforting descriptions of death. On the other side of this watershed they divine the presence of a reservoir of events that cannot be understood by the intelligence or prefigured by the imagination. Yielding to the fatal illusions of boredom, they end up conceiving of death as a new kind of life, a life composed of the least familiar parts of the universe and the metamorphoses that the intelligence will be capable of when she is liberated at last from the body, which is about as useful to her as a dog in a game of ninepins. Death will be a life in which total exercise of the intelligence will no longer be limited by the boredom and demands of the body, which loves the life of the flesh and delights in the physical world. Still later, they get to thinking about angels.

In six months I pass through these deadly stages. Fortunately my idle body and my instincts cannot adapt to mental calculations, to art for art's sake. I hate this life. I begin to desire a human state that would be the exact opposite of suffocating abstraction. I try to imagine free men who want to be—in reality, and not in dreams like Christians and bankers—everything it is given man to be.

I realize every day how puerile was the fear that possessed us in Paris. The acts we were expected to perform—acts that would be consistent with our families' status, with common courtesy, and with the abstract functions of the bourgeois world—were so empty and absurd that we thought all acts were eternally sterile, like the nuns who drink herb teas to make their breasts flow, and that men must always die in the dark. When we slept we had dreams that should have shown us the truth, but our masters were powerful enough to forbid dreams from breaking into the daylight. Hence our attempts at escape, which we thought were so dramatic. We didn't notice that everyone was happy to see us depart and encouraged us to go. All these people who gave us advice only wanted to disarm us, and they very nearly succeeded. Was there anyone who did not praise the various forms of retreat: profundity, confession, introspection, certain types of poetry, billiards, religion, the movies, adventure stories, the

tabloids, the exploits of famous aviators? Novelists who wrote
about inner adventures and psychologists who described conversion were held in high esteem; young men and petty clerks were
congratulated on creating fantasy lives for themselves—that was
called, for example, the Past Recaptured. It was even suggested
that Buddhism was charming. Meanwhile our masters were
easy in their minds; as long as you are busy with remembrance
of things past you are no threat to anyone. To flee meant that
you had no intention of taking a close look at the world you were
fleeing, that you were not going to call anyone to account on the
day you understood what it was all about. Go play and don't
bother the grown-ups. It was a wonderful plan for making us
forget about present evils and their remedies. Any examination
of the present imperils Order. You think you are innocent if
you say, "I love this woman and I want to act in accordance
with my love," but you are beginning the revolution. Besides,
your love will not succeed. What a sin it is to demand freedom
and announce that you want to do something to achieve it!
You will be driven back: to claim the right to a human act is to
attack the forces responsible for all the misery in the world.
The demands of man are simple. The day I began to think about
them I thought I was Columbus, or Newton; anyway, they are
more important than the business about the egg* or infinitesimal
calculus. Because they prophesy the ruin of the world. If anyone
stood in a public square in Paris and declared that men must live
like human beings, that plants live like plants and it's about
time men had a right to do the same, he would disappear under
a black heap of policemen. Simple demands: all you have to do

---

* An allusion to a popular French anecdote that tells how Columbus used
an egg to confound envious critics who said it had taken no great wit to
discover the new world. It had been a simple matter, they declared, the
only trick was to think of looking for it in the first place. Columbus is
supposed to have replied by taking an egg and asking which of the company could make it stand on end. When everyone objected that the feat
was impossible, Columbus crushed one end of the egg just enough to
flatten it and stood it on the table, rebuking his enemies with the words,
"That too was simple—one had only to think of it." (Trans.)

is ship the fables back to those who invent them and allow to flourish all the human capacities that ask only to exist without giving dialectical justifications every five minutes.

Will I have to content myself with lying in bed and imagining human life, outside of time? Must I be satisfied to fall back on that nonsense of the inner life again? Will I never be asked what human life would be made of and what it would be like? I do not see it clearly yet. I am groping my way—it's like trying to catch a pigeon flying about in a dovecote at twilight. But I know it is there and that I must draw aside the veils that hide it. The desert of stones and thoughts is fading out. I declare that despite the false prophets, there are objects and acts that are as natural as horses, that are located in times and places accessible to human beings. The cleverest tricks of what you madmen call your souls could never so much as imitate them. You can keep what is merely possible. We will have to handle tools, look after the living, cancel out the dead, and get to know our bodies at last; we will have to kill our enemies, teach children to walk, invent objects, laugh, learn about the world.

Action can call upon allies that are very different from all your algebras: abilities, needs, possessions. We must do everything to conciliate these natural allies whose voices you try to smother—with all your tricks and cunning precautions—under the heavy draperies of sound logic and sacred business morality. These allies are easier to love than the tales told by you bourgeois traitors would have us believe. They are so close to us that languages have no names for them: they have not yet become involved in human relations.

Did I have to go to the tropical deserts to unearth such ordinary truths? Did I have to go to Aden to seek out the secrets of Paris? On my return I found that many others had seen them as they gazed into the depths of the Seine. But I have no regrets. These truths have stared me in the face, they were revealed in such a dazzling light that I am certain never to lose them. I was too near my end to regard them as the errors of youth. No one will ever make me believe that growing up is the answer to everything.

I still think the chances of my coming upon these truths within the walls of the Latin Quarter were slim. They were getting ready to throw so many blankets over me: I might have been a traitor, I might have suffocated.

XIII

Let no one ever paint for me again the alluring picture of poetic voyages offering salvation, with their marine backgrounds, their different countries piled up one behind the other, and their strangely dressed figures standing in front of forests, mountains, peaks covered with eternal snows, and houses thirty stories high.

I know the truth about the sort of travel people were talking about in France between 1920 and 1927. It was a paler version of the old Christian determination to be dead to the world, to renounce the world in exchange for the most solemn promises of God, who spoke of a new creation, a new setting in which all life would be completely made over. What a profusion of visions, surprises, and incidents revealed, what an abundance of divinity.

And I ran straight into the arms of the very people who had frightened me. That is what it means to go from Scylla to Charybdis.

One could turn that into a reason for being perpetually afraid, for being perpetually the Wandering Jew.

But I am a Frenchman and a peasant: I love fields, I even love a single field, I would be content with that for the rest of my days, if neighbors passed by sometimes. I do not want to know the hopelessness of vagabonds—I found out what that was too, on the coasts of the Red Sea and the Indian Ocean, in the Nile delta and elsewhere. From time to time I had to fight off the desire to move on by trying to think of Aden as my field, even though the effort defied common sense.

Reef for reef, I'll take the land.

I reject sea voyages and itineraries. You always have the feeling that you are standing on a peak with great, steep slopes dropping away from you in all directions, and that you are going to roll down and lose yourself at the bottom. Everything is wrenched from you. You arrive at a port and you go ashore, hoping to possess a town and its inhabitants: not a chance! The boat sails off again and once more you have lost a human place and a fine opportunity to sit still. That is what it really means to travel: like a guilty man in Hades, you stretch out your arms and enfold only the smoke of ships, the mists of light. Travel is a series of irrevocable losses.

Let us give up trying to conquer the desirable archipelagos rich in oil and spices, where poets tell us tall women stand in colored robes, the sisters of Ariadne gathering the fruits of the sea and watching for the descendants of Theseus. In 1926 I heard some businessmen talking about the meeting of Solomon and the Queen of Sheba, about the Realm of Balkis and the Spice Coast. They were sincerely moved, they believed these places were at their doorstep. It is even possible that some archaeologist who responds to the element of the fantastic in his science will one day set out in search of Ophir, "between Aden and Dafar."

Let Ariadne rest in peace—*I* shall not condemn myself to the hell of travel. My enemies cannot count on my being so naive.

Finally, there is much to be learned from the elementary proposition that there are men everywhere, even in the capitals of the desert. I have covered many a sea-mile to find out why I feared my compatriots instead of loving them. How simple it all is at bottom! There are children, sensitive women, and even respectable men like doctors and notaries, who go walking alone at night: for many reasons, profound or frivolous, that do not concern me at the moment. They may see a tree, a tree that is just a tree, with branches and leaves, a trunk, bark—a willow with nests in it, night birds, and perhaps a shadow, if the moon is out. They may take it for a spectre who wants their soul, or a bandit who is going to rape the woman, rob the man, or kidnap the child; they may flee as if a train were coming down upon them. But they could take a close look and find that a branch deformed by the night is only a branch, and that they have as much right to climb on it as on a branch seen in the daytime.

I have gone a long way only to come back at last to the branch that frightened me so. I have come upon the same terrifying shadows I was fleeing and I see that they are men, and that the only reason they might be dangerous is that there are so many of them. I take their measure close up: they have the same dimensions and the same forms as in France. But the night that made them terrifying—that night of legends, of formal learning, of words, and fine arts—has been dissipated by the sun that dries up everything, even the dead. How insubstantial they are! No wonder I was afraid to be like them!

That is the reward for putting in at one port after another. There is only one valid kind of travel, and that is the journey toward men. It is the voyage of Ulysses, as I should have known if my study of the humanities hadn't been wasted. And its natural end is the return. The whole value of the voyage lies in its last day.

As for poetry, that last mineral element of travel, let it sink into the oblivion of the seas.

There is no wisdom in landscapes. There are writers who talk about the lessons to be learned from nature; they pretend to believe that stones and sky are teachers who speak in sign language and that men can imitate the attitudes and moral virtues of a city, a territory, or a zone of vegetation: serenity, intelligence, grandeur, despair, sensuousness.

But serious travelers have not set much store by this rhetoric. The travels of Montaigne are dry; Descartes' are stripped of everything, he is hardly even interested in men.

A man is not an eye that sees or an ear that listens. The earth has had nothing to do with the complexities that men have added to it in various places by centuries of civilization. It lies there without a word, ready for whatever men may make of it. It is a receptacle, a ball of wax; we must not mistake the imprints left by man for properties of the virgin wax.

Once you have stated that there are places in which you die of cold and others in which you dry up with the heat, and that it is only possible to live easily between the two, there is not much more to be said about the poetry of the earth. Landscapes are not associates, or professors of morals, or missionaries preaching order in one place and disorder in another: everything is inside ourselves. Landscapes have no powers of persuasion. That lyrical idea of nature is completely void of content.

Your wanderings will only bring you back to the order or disorder of the human flocks that inhabit the earth, and you will be forced to judge, to love, to hate, to yield, to resist: man awaits man—indeed that is his only intelligent occupation. Then you will not confuse the sense of well-being that you have in the country with communion, or the mixture of colors with inspirations of divine grace. You must not think you are saved because you are happy at the sight of green wheat: the families who go to Nogent-sur-Marne for a Sunday picnic exhaust everything there is in nature that can really touch the heart.

You may talk as long as you please about what man does on these revolving stages, and chances are I will understand you. A human judgment is the only intelligible one, even if it is a judgment about the earth. A melancholy landscape is one in which children die of hunger; a tragic landscape is one that is crossed by lines of helmeted police and convoys of cannons; an exalting landscape is one in which anybody can kiss a woman without trembling with cold or fear. This is the only thing I understand: that countries offer varying degrees of resistance to human desires and human joy. If I can live like a man in the four elements, any country will do—first let me breathe. The love of beauty may well come over me when I am old. But you make me laugh with your natural revelations and your storehouses of symbols. Why should I abandon hope in human intercourse and go lock myself up in nature? Why should I trust nature rather than living men? A man to whom love, or friendship, or victory had been denied, a man in utter despair, might be driven to such a retreat. This wisdom that no longer contains the slightest hope in man is the wisdom of Epicurus—when everything seemed lost, that hero jettisoned his cargo in order to save the sinking ship. Why do you want to see me in utter despair, abandoning myself to the movements of the sky? I am a harder nut to crack than you think.

Once I had understood what men are, I could think of only one thing: to go back. I was as impatient as a horse, with its great black eyes and anxious feet. I saw my time slipping away, this thing that belonged to me. Like all men, I am not rich in time: I am going to die. My isolation prevented me from taking any meaningful action, nothing I could do here would have the slightest effect in the West. Also, I suspected that in Europe I would not have to fight alone.

We can give joy only to someone whom we know, and love is the perfection of knowing. The same is true of hate. Among all the enemies of man, none was more familiar to me than France: it was France that, within the limits of my strength, I could hurt the most. There are so many ways to hurt someone when you know his lies, his vanities, the vulnerable parts of his body. Finally, I now thought of Europe in another way than I had before I left it. Europe is not a corpse, it is a tree trunk that has put out adventitious roots all around it, like a banyan tree. We must attack the trunk first: everyone is dying in the shade of its leaves.

XIV

Too slowly to suit my impatient mood, I come back. I was about to say, I come back up: we think we are thinking about the universe, but we are only thinking about maps, and to go from south to north one reads a map from the bottom up. In the sky, that is meaningless: north is in all directions.

Another voyage delayed every day by winds and by the loading and unloading of merchandise. Between Massawa and Jidda we have to make our way through the whirling, stinging gusts of a blinding white storm. We slow down to five knots; I eat some Chinese bananas given me by an Arab merchant from Hodeida, I smell the sheep in the hold. I am drunk with impatience and fury—are the very winds to be sent against me?

The cities half buried in sand, heaped up behind lines of coral, signal to us, but the signals immediately disappear. It is a horrible, rushing film consisting of one eclipse after another, and it leaves fading memories.

Zeila is one of the ports on the coast of British Somaliland. They say it was also a port of the Queen of Sheba. It is about sixty miles southeast of Djibouti.

It is only a straggling village, no higher above sea level than a raft. From the bridge of a ship it is a sort of faded mirage, not at all one of those tall, sunlit apparitions that dominate the watery plain like great galleys covered with pennants, bell-turrets, and masts, but an image eroded by sand, high winds, and sun.

Since the open sea is separated from the shoreline by insidious shallows whose twists and turns must be followed on the navigation charts, ships stay out to sea. First the passengers go down onto a little native *boutre* that leans over the water even when there is no wind. The black sailors crouch in the bow, impatient to touch the coast with their hands. Then the *boutre* scrapes bottom. You are carried in a chair by two tall Somalis who thread their way through the back passages as through a familiar maze.

Young boys run and the sea leaps up; they shout, under a shower of copper water that streams over their skin, the beautiful black skin with red reflections typical of the country. Their shouts fly up to the sky and never come down again.

The ground is like a mortar filled with dead fish: at every step you crush fishbones and shells, raising a dust mixed with scales.

The cry of a child, the querulous voice of an old woman, the bleating of a sheep whose throat is being cut behind a wall; no sound of steps, no rustling of leaves, no songs, no arguments. A boundless silence falls from the sky, like a rain of ashes shot up by some volcano more distant than the cry of a lark.

You see groups of people sleeping in empty squares. In white, unfurnished rooms, idle traders buy and sell a few skins. They smoke the *Elephant* or *Scissors* cigarettes which Wills manufactures for the colored people and which a white man does not smoke. Do the men of Zeila feed on stones? Do they feel forgotten on the edge of their desert? Do they live underground in order to accustom their bodies to the huge weight of death?

At Hodeida, the port serving Sana, Manakha, and upper Yemen, in the warehouses, at the far end of long corridors, behind carved folding doors, lie heaped the verdant hills of coffee beans where, as in a cold bath, one's limbs would lose their sweat. The little Jewish women who have come down from their mountains of Sana screen the coffee. They wear garments of faded blue linen and, in the desert wind, they bite on a wet corner of red and black cloth. Under their filth, what desire they could arouse! For lack of time, these desires disintegrate in the sun.

It is April, the time of year when the pilgrims come up to Yenbo and Jidda, the ports for Medina and Mecca. Near Luhaiya we meet transports loaded with Malayans and Indians, calm voyagers on the oily waters, who see holiness at the end of their journey. They possess cotton umbrellas, metal trunks painted with flowers, and troops of children wearing golden caps. They have to have leisure to await the pleasure of the quarantines, the offices, the Customs, the Egyptian doctors with their shrill politeness. Assembled under the windy, open sheds of the ports, they mint a small fortune in patience. In the same way, in the city of Jidda itself, which is full of crumbling sections of wall, rubble from excavations, and heaps of plaster from demolished buildings, on the side toward the Gate of Mecca and the Tomb of the Mother of Mankind, there wait caravans of loaded camels, and sordid Fords dating from the early comedies of Mack Sennett. Hope is in the air, amid the sort of torpor that accompanies an illness. The pilgrims endure everything, the brutalities, the delays, being robbed by the pilgrimage contractors. All that's missing is the blue canteens, the plaster Bernadettes, the medals of the Virgin, and the students of Polytechnique acting as stretcher-bearers, and you'd think you were at Lourdes.

Flags hang down their staffs like skins. They are the pennants of the European consulates, of countries with Moslem subjects. They make you think of a Geneva of Islam: for once the red flag of the Soviets is willing to be in the same company with the murderous Union Jack. But the consuls are asleep behind their closed grillwork balconies in every corner of this city without ice, where the violet-syrup is served at room temperature, as if it were medicine.

In the port, between two rows of coral, the white yacht of King Ibn Saud is rusting away on a copper sulphate sea.

Patience and sleep are the two passwords of these inconsolable lands adorned with sinister wonders and peopled by ominous men. There is an Arabic poem in which the Arab says, "I am the Son of Patience." These oriental cities are drying out in the sun like a fish stranded on a beach, or a corpse lying in the germless air of the desert. It is a sterile corruption. The inhabitants, who seem countless in the midst of this empty wasteland, stir only faintly. Engaged in activities from which all meaning has evaporated, they sit on stones that have fallen from their houses and let themselves slip toward death. They exist in a kind of speechless beatitude from which they emerge periodically to talk rapidly and sign business papers.

In the ideas he forms about life, a European is never able to separate human actions from refreshing views of vegetation, rivers, and machines. He is the grandson of peasants and crafts-men: an uneasiness that cannot be dissipated by the most rea-sonable arguments grips him when he is faced with an existence devoted to inexplicable tasks—tasks that are not measured in the last analysis by the growth of a harvest or the production of a tool —and to leisure activities that do not normally include a walk in a garden.

Between his life and the life of growing things there is an easy and continuous exchange. The changing seasons, which are as real to him as plants, serve as his landmarks. His recreation and his rest periods are seasonal, even his religious holidays. Each of the four seasons brings different work and different pleasures. The city dweller is not excluded from these laws, he has only to see the chestnut trees break into leaf and the first cherries appear in the fruit markets. He is able to master the modest forces of his climate, and he therefore entertains the illusion that nature is docile and perhaps his ally, and that he can bend it to his own purposes. In the temperate zones of earth, man thinks he is free because he triumphs.

And the European is a mechanic. The invention, use, and understanding of instruments and machines occupy those hours which are not ultimately connected with the productive earth. Each of these operations also gives him proof of his power. The idea of fatalism does not come naturally to him. These acts may yet save the people of Europe.

But in the desert regions, the earth does not participate in the production of things that are useful to life, and the only relations men have with it are either too mysterious or too simple. It is a place for never varying walks, an object for monotonous con-templation. Between the Sinai Peninsula and the Island of Soco-tra, you have to accept an environment in which men are truly aliens. They are powerless, their wishes and desires do not shake the permanence of the desert. The natural phenomena, the sandstorms and rainstorms, take on such violence as to preclude any human attempt to resist them or to make use of them. Be-cause there are no rivers, no wheat, and too much wind, you find no windmills. It is on this impotence that the belief in fatalism is based. A man who can love a waterfall and at the same time set up a turbine on it is not going to believe that all things are written.

So these lost cities infect a European with a sort of disease of laziness. Rejected, forgotten, they consume themselves, and life takes on the guise of death. Do not talk to the people of Europe about *kief* or *nirvana*. They will tell you to leave the dead alone.

At last the Mediterranean reappears, peopled with all the drowned men of ancient times.

One morning, having come full circle, I saw the Château d'If and, against a background of white hills, Notre Dame de la Garde. I got what I asked for—the first two symbols that were waiting to meet me were precisely the two most revolting objects on earth: a church and a prison.

XV

*France who nourished me with the milk of thy breast . . .**

Here, once again, is France. I am coming closer. Every turn of the propeller lessens the distance. Passage through the islands, view of Marseille, Customs officers. I recognize the familiar face of a nation: I was born and raised here, like Brer Rabbit in his briar patch.

I have not seen so much as Ulysses, but here is my wanderer's Ithaca, where no faithful wife awaits me. I have passed through cities, but the same men were living everywhere. When the traveler returns, he has had time, during all those white-hot days and all those nights of rumination under the fans, to draw up his accounts in full. The settling of those accounts is not necessarily so lively, prompt, and joyous as the one in the *Odyssey*. When I read about that brawl I used to think it was the most exalting fate that could be prophesied to a man:

"And Odysseus peered all through the house, to see if any man was yet alive and hiding away to shun black fate. But he found all the sort of them fallen in their blood in the dust, like fishes that the fishermen have drawn forth in the meshes of the net into a hollow of the beach from out the gray sea, and all the fish, sore longing for the salt sea waves, are heaped upon the sand, and the sun shines forth and takes their life away; so now the wooers lay heaped upon each other."

In the salon of an ocean liner, decorated like a pharaoh's burial chamber (and all the actors from the Comédie Française and all the officials' wives were overflowing with gratitude to the Messageries Maritimes), I recognized France from her portrait. With

---

* A quotation slightly adapted from a celebrated sonnet by the sixteenth century poet Joachim du Bellay, in which France is praised as "mother of the Arts, and Arms, and Laws." (Trans.)

all her vices showing in the charming, conventional designs to which our knowledge of the earth is reduced. There are people whose portraits reveal the evil that is in them. On a geographical map, France was spread out, petty and avaricious, between her seas, her mountains, and her Rhine. A locked box. The borders assigned by chance geological formations and prehistoric cataclysms that would one day be profitable to the future land barons and steel merchants who were still sleeping in the recesses of a great ape—these borders have been the pretext for France's ample share in the history of assassinations and cowardly deeds and for the few military glories that adorn the last homilies of Marshals of France who have re-enlisted in the Académie Française. This piece of ground is enough for her politicians, for the angry old men who rule her destiny, for the great patriots who feed on corpses, for all the grave-robbers who prop up the bodies of dead Frenchmen and try to save them from final putrefaction. A smell of embalming floats everywhere. How can you expect anyone to take seriously people who never see beyond five hundred thousand square kilometers?

This country peopled by slave-drivers and obedient slaves, to whom the length of their chains—shortened every day—still gives the illusion of freedom and the semblance of power, is surrounded by the sea. She does nothing with it. She is afraid her sons might get their feet wet and catch cold. "Jean, stay in the village." On summer evenings the song echoes across every public square in the provinces. For the masters of the French, the ocean is a reservoir of defenses, an excuse for guns, submarines, and cruisers. Be tempted by freedom? Who speaks of temptation? Does anyone assume the charming voice of the Spirit of Evil to seduce the stammering Fausts in their provincial towns? We would be invaded. The French cannot abide the song of the sirens.

France is the victim of dreams of impenetrability. Oh to have frontiers made of diamond and corundum! But only, alas, these borders of water, granite, and shale.

Still dirty with the excrement and filth of her war, she groans about her poverty, her dignity, her spiritual mission, and the smallness of her profits and the greatness of her good will. For she is led by hypocritical businessmen who hide the profits shown on their balance sheets and weep over the hardness of the times. They repeat in her name that she is the intellectual capital of the world, the eldest daughter of the Church, the muse of democracy: thus do they nourish with illusions the people whom the accidents of marriage, love, and travel have made French. A hungry man has many ears.* Thus do they delude the people on the other side of the border, who sleep, they say, in dreadful beds that are not shaped like our beds.

By France I mean the band of men who possess the land, the mines, quarries, factories, mills, and buildings, the masters of men. I am justified in identifying them with France since they always claim to be the only ones who have the right to speak in her name. This is not the time to speak of their victims, of the agricultural workers and the laborers, the soldiers, office clerks, and tie salesmen, of the girls who have had abortions, of the men and women to whom France does not belong.

Incidentally, France is not a person, as the statues by Dalou might lead school children to believe. One must not imagine that she is a personage of supernatural size, with birds on her head, walking inside the walls that enclose her domain, a kind of great queen bee, mother of forty million children. France is a collection of men, products, and events.

I do not like these men, or their products, or their events. Let no one try to make me ashamed because I am insulting a goddess. Eternal visage—eternal mistress of generals. I have not been disrespectful to this non-existent virgin.

France possessed, possessors of France, French possessors, possession of France—word games.

Not one of these possessors is missing. They flock to my call like the seagulls that used to crowd around me long ago, on the day I arrived in vacation country. Not one is absent among those

---

* A reversal of the French proverb which says, "A hungry man has no ears," i.e. it is useless to preach to him. (Trans.)

petty bourgeois of whom I was one, with their clean collars that used to be starched but are soft now so as to give them a false, American elegance, with their black suits—eternal mourning for anybody: a cardinal, a wife, an uncle, a terrier—with their bowlers, their soft felt hats, and their Sunday canes. Not one of their wives is missing, the idle ones and the domestic ones, who march through love like a cavalry squadron through a wheat field, and not a single blade is left standing. Not one of their poor prostitutes in uniform, of their children strangled by the wisdom of their fathers. Not one of those correct countenances that cannot quite dissolve in their morning washbasins the traces of pride, or cowardice, or boredom. I walk, and I see to my right and to my left, before me and behind me, my former brothers who were the compost heap in which I grew, the rich plant layer of businessmen, professors, senators, traveling salesmen, industrialists, lawyers, officers. Readers of books. Men who spend a month at the seashore, who are ashamed to have syphilis but are all indulgence for gonorrhoea, who detest love and respect marriage, men who see their own portrait in the newspapers every morning in millions of copies.

I recognize their smallest gestures, and not one of them can move me; I am in the least moving of nations. I understand the titles on the backs of books, the street cries, the word "Radical" and the word "Mind." A French citizen comes back with me, or rather, there was a double waiting for me in Marseille and he fell into step with me. I am going to do everything possible to lose him. He represents everything that fell away from me when the name of my province was Hadhramaut.

Arabia-France, Aden-Paris, Versailles-Lahej, the names of countries and cities are henceforth interchangeable; I feel I could just as well say Paris-New York, London-Melbourne. The Place de l'Opéra coincides exactly with the Victoria Crescent, the offices of my relatives and friends are identical to the offices of the Anglo-Indian firms, the Clignancourt barracks to those of the Second Devon. The people I pass at the subway exit at six o'clock coming up out of those mouths, like Orpheus in a daze, have the same dangling arms, the same gray foreheads, the same mechanical bodies as the companions with whom I used to go to the club toward the end of the afternoon in Aden.

Aden taught me that I would understand everything in my native country. But I take no pride in an intelligence that is capable of comprehending how a phonograph works: nothing is easier to understand than a model that you can take apart. That is how a child discovers all the mysteries of the human body inside a cardboard corpse: he lifts a lid and unhooks the heart, a second lid and the transverse colon comes away in his hands.

The French live out the days of their interminable lives like snails inside shells so heavy that they cannot cross the great deserts that separate them from action and thought. With all the cunning of old men who hold annuities, they see to it that nothing happens among them. Not even those encounters between automobiles bristling with machine guns that are the Americans' last resort for social entertainment.

The French are bodies overrun by parasites and by the residue of memory. Curled up in bed, they ruminate on what has happened in the past and what is yet to come. They project into the future profits that they know by heart, the advantages of piety, of professional conscientiousness, service in the reserves, school friendships, whore houses. Thrifty accountants making calculations in corners. Thrifty lovers satisfying themselves alone in corners. They flee one another, they hate one another, they live together like strangers. They are never anything but accomplices. To really come close to another person is as frightening to them as a descent into hell. Do not speak to them of friendship; they prefer séances with a medium. If they love a woman, they want to dominate her like a laborer, possess her like a pair of gloves.

Their thinkers have manufactured for their use antiseptic models of man. You learn to take them apart at school, and this exercise relieves you of the necessity for real understanding and effective love. Indeed, you are very pleased that you know so much about man, more than you need to know for business purposes, and after all, these abstract descriptions suffice for what man has become. They constitute what is called Culture.

The French are in their burrows, defending their property at all times against surrounding property owners, and Property in general against those who possess nothing. France, the country of lawsuits over boundary walls. Everywhere steel traps, vicious dogs, barbed wire, pieces of glass, broken bottles, civil code: if there is one thing they really like it's the sign "No Trespassing."

All my relatives, all my cousins, all my boyhood friends belong to this species of human beings who live out sterile lives being respectful and receiving tips.

Exceeded in power and dignity by those whom they themselves call the great bourgeoisie, wedded to the destiny of that class and united with it, they carry out its orders to oppress a vast proletariat that is emerging from unconsciousness as from a night, and that carries with it the last hope of mankind. They are paid for this Holy Alliance in profits, for which they have invented special names. The members of this delicate species reject the words used to designate the reward for the real labor of workers and peasants. Since they pretend that their work is a spiritual mission, they have words to distinguish themselves from mercenary people who work only so that they may eat. They receive salaries, fees, emoluments, and compensation, but not wages or pay. Comes at last the glorious day when they receive a dividend; they know they have finally crossed the imaginary line that separated them from perfect complicity. With the only sincere emotion it is given them to feel, they can now pronounce the religious word "capital." Now the only difference between their masters and themselves is one of degree; essentially they are the same. Whether you have one share or a thousand, the number no longer matters. All their baseness, all their weighty power, all their lack of humanity, comes from this crossing of the line. It is no longer their lives they are defending but a luxurious profit and the idea it gives them of their own importance—the amount of the profit is irrelevant. It can even make them cruel. They sacrifice everything for the order that guarantees them this profit and ensures the permanence of their mystical transformation from workers into *rentiers*. Even though the profit provides no concrete satisfaction. A profit buys objects, it can only manifest itself through a purchase. These purchases are dead. The objects are no sooner possessed than they are threadbare: they breed the sickness of false desires. In order for a man to enjoy his profits, in order for him to be conscious of them, he must change them into visible proof of his solitude and power. The simplest satisfactions are perceptible to him only at the moment when they require the expenditure of profit. The bourgeois does not go to the clinic for treatment; he prefers to pay his doctor. It pains him that the woman he loves doesn't cost him anything; he wants to pay for her. His only goal is to dominate by purchasing power, which means that the buyer is envied and crushes other men. It doesn't matter how limited this power is. Thus their contempt for others and the envy they inspire are the emotions that fill their lives. They feel they are alive only when someone is jealous of them, or hates them. They content themselves with that, because after all you do have to feel you are alive, to feel you exist. No one is satisfied with boredom. I say they are bored because their real life has been killed and is beyond recall. Men are not like crabs: their amputated limbs do not grow back automatically.

Reality dissolved. An existence of smoke. Dreamlike passions. Man has quietly become an entry in the account of profits and losses, and no one has noticed the change.

Real work and real possession do exist—among peasants, craftsmen, and poets, to whom possession means the unity of action, reward, and product. But the bourgeois produce and possess abstractly. Since they long ago inherited the land of Israel, they spend their lives lending at interest. They are financiers, big or little; they own bonds and receive abstract sums paid by abstract debtors—a city, a company, a state, a railroad. Or they own shares: workers of flesh and blood labor in order to prolong the existence of these phantoms. Between them and living creatures, between them and human life, stands the bank with its fantastic retinue of stock exchanges, brokers, and salesmen. The bourgeois type of possession and profit separates them from everything real. They live in a world of magic, and their only contact with the real world is through weird long-distance signals. The day when these people hold in their hands a legal power of attorney or a green stock certificate, they partake of the mystical nature of a nonexistent being. They receive the host of capital.

They do not exist. They are driven by the demons of abstraction. What do they think? Who is aware of their existence? Registry offices and catalogs. They have as many labels as an old suitcase. In order to be able to sleep easy, they lock up all their collections of signs and symbols: a marriage certificate, a military record, a voter's registration card, and all the froth of paper that the circulation of money leaves in men's houses.

All the monuments of France defend the magical state of these men. At every cardinal point their sheltered life is protected against other men's attempts to live in the open air. It is impossible to breathe, you are at the bottom of a well. I know why I felt I was suffocating; it is no longer an obscure suffocation, the blind, struggling movement of a dream, but mutilation under the sun, asphyxiation in broad daylight. With a fine audience to watch me suffocate. Everything around me belongs to my enemies. I have nothing, I enjoy nothing. Everywhere I see the stone proofs of their domination: the churches, the national monuments, the barracks, the institutes, the police stations, the courthouses, brothels, ministries. You cannot stretch out your arms without your fingers touching the door of a bank, or the chest of a policeman or a Knight of the Legion of Honor. Can I set free the woman I love? They put a spoke in the wheel of love. From every direction they rush to the spot where a word of protest is heard, where an attempt at deliverance is being made. When they withdraw they leave the sidewalk bare: their police, their idle onlookers, and their sages act with the mindless certainty of machines. What does a vertical tower think about? What does Officer 36541 think about? What does Monsieur Bergson think about?

No wonder you are strangled, in this country full of the different species, varieties, and families of *Homo Economicus*.

A long time ago, when scholars sitting in their armchairs began to describe the appearance and habits of *Homo Economicus,* many people did not take them at their word and called real man to witness against abstract man. No one could realize at the time that these professors were simply describing the new abstract existence of humanity and were the first to point out the eclipse of real man. No one suspected that their description seemed abstract only because it was the faithful reflection of an abstract model.

In the beginning, *Homo Economicus* was as simple and single as a triangle. All the examples of him were as alike as pins. But he had descendants, he has given birth to families that do not always love each other, even though they have a common ancestor. *Homo Economicus* is now a banker, an industrialist, a police commissioner, a broker. There are different varieties of him— some are *rentiers*, some are small landowners, others play the market. You may meet a *Homo Economicus* who is a civil servant, or even a worker. He is an animal that is happy to be able to save its surplus profit. Although, with his fondness for maxims, he is always saying you can't get something for nothing, he has this profit without giving anything for it in exchange. He prizes it all the more because he really gets it free. He has the body of a man. Neither dogs and horses, nor women, nor the Angel of Death realize that he is merely a caricature of a man; he loves, he eats, he digests, he eliminates with a man's organs, he closes his eyes at night, he can walk. But despite these appearances, he is more like a slot machine, he is a piece of apparatus that walks and talks, no more human than a lamp that lights up or a motor that starts when the switch is turned on. It is possible that the lamp thinks it is lighting up voluntarily, and that a steering wheel does not turn without an agreeable awareness that it is rotating of its own free will.

Homo Economicus crushes underfoot the last remaining men, he is opposed to the last of the living and wants to convert them to his death. The great trick of the bourgeoisie is to make the workers shareholders or *rentiers*: they are then won over to the morality, the hardness, and the death of *Homo Economicus*. Will men eternally let themselves be trampled on and taken in by the talking machines? It is time to destroy *Homo Economicus*: he can be wounded, he is as vulnerable as a man, when he is naked. But there is no hope of persuading him—he does not know that he is crushing you or why he does it: capital requires him to crush, it is like a god-given law. Capital gives him enough passion, enough feeling to enable him to carry out his task with conviction; the passions themselves increase profits and returns. He does not mean to crush you, he does not give justifications for it. He is not admirable, or perfect, or blissful, because he crushes. *Homo Economicus* feels no joy, he derives no happiness from the misery of men. I do not see a judge with slaves standing on his left, and complete men, the supermen of France, on his right. No sacrifice brings beauty or joy to *Homo Economicus*: have you but looked at his pleasures, have you seen his face? It is impossible to find human justifications for the absurdity of his life and the deadliness of his power. You cannot fall back on Plato's arguments justifying slavery and degradation by the production of wise men who are really joyous and whose lives might weigh as much in the balance as the lives of ten thousand times ten thousand workers in chains. You are not living in the fifth century B.C. Nor even in the time of Christ. And anyway, that feeble sorcerer no longer protects anyone except steel merchants, owners of spinning mills, and rubber traders.

Homo Economicus has his illusion of happiness. He talks about his power, and he keeps men to manufacture illusions for him: novelists, historians, epic poets, philosophers. Because from time to time, when one of his organs isn't working properly, he feels that his life does not have the substance that life demands. So he plunges into imaginary satisfactions. Fortunately, he is a respectful animal who loves to hold things in veneration. *Homo Economicus* respects that which protects him. He is respectful on every level of society, all modern conveniences for the conscience on every floor. For example, he embraces with pretended enthusiasm the causes that have been invented to make his desert bearable: the law, duty, loyalty, charity, patriotism. There was a time when these words had weight, even though it is hard to believe that they once composed a human language and stood for things that men were willing to die for, which is the only proof of love. But they have been drained of meaning. They are empty shells that rattle against each other in the board rooms and cabinet meetings where politicians plot their mischief. *Homo Economicus* also respects great men. The existence of great men justifies his own existence. You should see the French on holidays, parading before the heroes who are wisely provided for their recreational needs, for the tricks their thinkers and their ministers perform like trained dogs, for the tricks the French perform before their Dead. And they call these tricks communion and life. You should see them when one of their little great men has died. They are at home in this sublime atmosphere of black drapes, flags, and sacred masses. They crowd to the place where the body lies in state, men, women, and little children eager for good examples. On such days there are great silent flocks of black sheep tended by the police; when evening comes and the traffic thins out, all you can hear is a damp shuffling as of guests invited to church for a wedding or a funeral. The faces carved out of soft stone never move their lips. The heads are bent. Every heart is filled with the rottenness called the Majesty of Death. There is a mysterious magnetic force by which they are drawn to corpses, like the files of insects that feed on the corpses of little animals— moles, weasels, rats. Poor in divinity, they feel lucky to have a dead man to worship before going back to work. They have nothing to get their teeth into. Except decaying carcasses. They nose out the ceremonious grief of important families who are at last brought down to the level of the anonymous multitudes. What ecstasy to walk between the wooden barriers, to lift your hat and repeat "In the name of the Father!" This contact re-charges them like old batteries. They delight in their dead gods, accessible at last, with their projecting teeth, their sunken cheeks, and their chin straps.

And then there are the patriotic holidays, the exalting spectacle of machine guns and cannons, which are more poetic than breasts, the national holidays when only their dignity prevents them from picking up the first girl they pass in the street. There are the horse races. The marriages. The social events. Again, at all levels—at the Cercle Interallié or at the druggist's in Tours, or at Charles L.–Dreyfus's.*

That's all they can think of for amusement, that and the books of Anatole France and Paul Valéry. And the theatres. The paintings. When the days of communion are over, they sink back into their barren lives, without even having realized the common, everyday truth: that men and women have bodies, arms that jostle the crowd, faces to love. It never occurs to them that there were men at Foch's funeral, women at the Armistice Day celebration, arms and legs at the Cercle Interallié. They still do not know that on a holiday, at even the humblest celebration, they might make something of the chance encounters that call forth only their muttered abuse or their polite civilities.

With all their profits they are poor. As poor as the men I love, as poor as I myself. The prison guards are almost as bored as the prisoners, the sergeants are not much more joyous than their men. But they wear masks when they look at themselves in the mirror. They don't see how bad they look behind the gilt cardboard. But we, we have no masks, we see our abasement, our indigence and misery, we know that we are mutilated, nothing cheats our hunger, we do not suck on pebbles to forget our thirst and pretend it is slaked. Their destiny, their way of life, and the procession of their years are based on our annihilation.

Their life is sustained by the pride they take in it, by a vilely deformed and distended self-love. Pride prevents them from recognizing that they are impatient with their poverty, that they need diversion and legends. In Aden, people postponed the diversion and legends until the time when they would return to Europe. Here they put false, proud food into their mouths, they crush with pride, they occasionally dispense proud charity, they sit down to eat and lie down to sleep in proud rooms, they read and go to the theatre with pride in understanding words and

---

* Cercle Interallié: a fashionable men's club in Paris. Charles Louis-Dreyfus: a large-scale shipowner, grain merchant and banker.

images which they alone have the leisure and education to comprehend. Their only compensation is that they possess what others lack. Pride is born of hatred for mankind and a taste for hurting others. They do not know that they like to exercise their evil powers, but crushing and humiliating are the only activities that make them aware of themselves. That is the only real power they have. If they feel pride, they are not like Beethoven the day he finished the choral symphony, or like Lenin the day he saw that the revolution was victorious, but like a monkey that has found an old top hat and put it on. These antics hide their misery. And *Homo Economicus* thinks he is satisfied with his fate, since he is envied by his poor relations. Let no one among the living waste his time describing to *Homo Economicus* how wretched and sterile he is. Epicurus did not seek to save the tyrants and the bankers, but craftsmen, slaves, and prostitutes. I have heard the way this machine laughs: it is easier to destroy it than to breathe human life into it. If one of our enemies discovers that he is confusing the froth with the sea, he will save himself on his own. But no appeal can make itself heard on the heights of that pride, or break down all that sediment of evil habits. If the last trickles of human sap have dried up in the vessels of these old trees, let no one try to do anything for them.

But their emptiness is not solely their own affair. They defend and preserve their misery and its causes, with guile, with violence, with obstinacy and skill. And their misery brings with it the misery of those who do not love nothingness, but life. I had good reason to be afraid: these mindless enemies are terrifying, they are full of night. I was afraid of both the lives they lead and the lives they make other men lead. Anonymous as the hangman's rope: the rope has neither desires nor joys, but it hangs. They shall not be justified. They shall be weighed, they and their souls. For they have souls.

The police, the government, ethics, justice, sin, punishment— these are the things that stir their thoughts. A soul is that which is not man's thing, but which comes from outside to dwell in him. To have a soul is to be possessed. It is time to exorcise these demons. Capital is a soul too. They have many more souls than I, they even have more souls than the men of Aden, because they have to defend themselves. In Aden no one questioned the sovereignty of economic man. No one accused him of being empty, no one denounced him as a murderer. Let us recognize that a revolutionary is a man who can get along without a soul. Or who doesn't need an official identity. I am perfectly willing to grow old under a number, if you like. All that nasty mess of abstract forces and ideas is the true cause of slavery and the confused fear it inspired in me. The hour grows late for me to strip bare and destroy these mannikins of skin and bones and calculations, that I took for invincible demons. It is time to make war on the causes of fear. Time to get one's hands dirty: there will be time enough to have brothers later. I am in a position to make war because I have been completely delivered from the fear that overtook me like an arrow, even in far off Arabia, where I had reason to think I was safe at last. It is no use running away. I am staying here: if I fight, fear vanishes. I have already won half the battle. I must pay attention and not forget anything. They are lying in wait in the depths of their comfortable lairs. The future that awaits us is not a tempting one: to become like them, with the shameful memory of having wanted, when we were young, to live like men; to become one of their servants, performing tasks which are assigned by them and completely laid out in advance. I was afraid of those ends, and there can be no others without a battle. I do not want to die degraded like a banker, or dragged down like a submissive laborer.

A banker and a laborer are the last elementary symbols that rise above the smoky horizon lit by the fires of Paris. All the reality of this world is like a caricature in *Pravda*. It is being played out on the stage of a gigantic puppet show built by the communists. There are no other characters left: the Master and the Journeyman, the Father and the Child, Ariel and Caliban have been relegated to the attic along with the forgotten figures of the Lord, the Monk, and the Serf. The poets, the politicians, and the philosophers think that this vision is too simple and crude and that one has to be more subtle. Let us have the courage to be crude: let us sweep the spirit of subtlety down the sewer along with the flags and the great warriors. There are only two human species left, and the only bond between them is hatred: the one that crushes and the one that does not consent to being crushed. There has never been any peace treaty, there is only war. Every minute should harbor a thought against our enemies: in 1913 the old men thought that continuously about Germany.

I am going to live among my enemies. To live perseveringly, that is to say not passively, not letting time lull me to sleep with the pleasant, lazy sound of its passage, but patiently, attentively, and angrily. I must have the virtue in which we have been most lacking: constancy. But it is easier to be constant in war than in poetry or in love. Poetry and women pass, but the revolution is never past.

You are solitary men. When you are dining, when you are in a theatre or a movie, when you are walking on the sidewalk, when you are in bed with a woman, look for traps. The settings through which you pass are enemy property: they are arrayed against you. You must destroy them. From the moment you awake until the moment you fall asleep, curled up in a bed as protective as a womb, you live among them; you must be like spies, you must nurse your anger and allow yourselves no respite. How can you penetrate their secrets unless you hate them?

There is nothing noble about this war. The adversaries in it are not equals: it is a struggle in which you despise your enemies, you who want to be men. Will you be forever sitting at your catechism? You will have to refuse them a glass of water when they are dying: they pay notaries and priests to attend them in death. They do not need men's help, they have the help of religion. We are talking about destruction, and not just a victory that leaves the enemy on his feet. It is a war that allows of no atonement. We are not living in the days of the feudal wars with their truces of God. We are not living in the days when Jacob wrestled with the angel. They say that in certain Greek cities the oligarchs took this oath: "I will be the people's adversary, and in the Council I will do them all the harm I can." Are you going to let your enemies be the only ones to swear such an oath?

Let none of our actions be free of anger. To take time out to breathe, or to take the night off, is to waste time, to delay the fight. Love alone is also an act of revolt, they crush love. If you find that your parents or your wives are in the enemy camp, you will abandon them.

I will no longer be afraid to hate. I will no longer be ashamed to be fanatic. I owe them the worst: they all but destroyed me. My hatred will be increased by anger at knowing that hatred is a diminution of Being, that it is a state born of poverty. Spinoza says that hate and repentance are the two enemies of mankind: at least I will not know repentance. I will be friends with hate. And with oblivion. The sacred duties implanted in men's hearts, the magical dramas stirred up inside them, are henceforth only the symbols of deadly games.

All that remains of travel is a series of chaotic images: the rout of the enemies of man, some disturbances on the surface of the earth, and a few men in black suits, with their arms stretched out on the pavement, in the middle of the deserted Place de la Concorde.